BODYGUARD…
TO BRIDEGROOM?

BODYGUARD...
TO BRIDEGROOM?

BY

NIKKI LOGAN

MILLS
BOON®

First published in Great Britain 2015
By Mills & Boon, an imprint of HarperCollins*Publishers*
1 London Bridge Street, London, SE1 9GF

Large Print edition 2016

© 2015 Nikki Logan

ISBN: 978-0-263-26182-0

Our policy is to use papers that are natural, renewable
and recyclable products and made from wood grown
in sustainable forests. The logging and manufacturing
processes conform to the legal environmental regulations
of the country of origin.

Printed and bound in Great Britain
by CPI Antony Rowe, Chippenham, Wiltshire

For Margaret Kruger
'White, no sugar, half a cup.'

And for the staff—and wildlife—
of Al Maha Desert Resort who offered me
such a transformative experience.

CHAPTER ONE

IT TOOK BRAD KRUGER all of three seconds to sift through the faces in the crowd of passengers disembarking from the pointy end of the flight from London and identify the one he needed. First, he filtered out anyone with a Y chromosome, then the women over forty or under eighteen, then the impeccably dressed locals returning to the pricey desert emirate of Umm Khoreem. That left only three priority passengers that could be his client and only one of them had her long hair out and flowing gloriously over bare shoulders.

There she was…codename 'Aspirin'—for the headache he was going to have for the next month.

Of all the gin joints in all the towns…

Brad glanced along the long row of immigration staff in their pristine robes and watched as Seraphina Blaise was subtly corralled to the entrance of a long, winding and empty queue that casually eased her away from the one filled with locals and towards a counter with double the staff. As she negotiated the maze of retractable belts, she seemed oblivious to the fact she'd just been selected for special immigration attention.

She might have left a British Christmas all rugged up, but somewhere over the Baltic she'd pared back into something more suited to a desert one—except that apparently she'd dressed for the heat rather than for the culture.

'Here we go...' Brad muttered under his breath, pushing off the ornately carved pillar he'd been leaning against and triangulating a course to bring him as close as possible to the official who'd flagged her.

Her inadequate dress had probably caught Immigration's attention, but it was her arrest record that would likely *keep it*. Umm Khoreem issued visas on arrival for those who were just visiting. No visa, no entry; and people had been refused entry into the security-conscious state on much less than bad fashion choices and a fresh conviction.

A carefully blank official took her passport as Brad drew closer on the Umm Khoreem side of the immigration barrier, asked a few questions, frowned at her answers, and spent the next few minutes reading various pages on his touch screen while the leggy brunette shuffled awkwardly before him. She glanced around to pass the time, and Brad saw the moment she finally registered that she'd ended up in a queue for one while everyone else was being whisked through further along.

Her rounded eyes swung back to the official.

Yep. Just you, love...

Her whole body changed then. She lost the casual lightness with which she'd practically bounced along the switchback lanes, her bare shoulders sagged and her spine ratcheted straight. Remembering her last run-in with authorities perhaps...

Brad caught the eye of one of the other immigration staff, who took his time sauntering over but bowed his cloaked head and listened as Brad briskly murmured his name, credentials and purpose. The man nodded and returned to his post, then picked up the telephone. At the next aisle, the first immigration officer answered, flicking his eyes up to his colleague and then over to where Brad now stood before returning his gaze to the woman in front of him. The official barely acknowledged him, but barely was all he needed.

Whatever happened from now he'd just insinuated himself within the process.

And he could do a much better job from within than from without.

The official requested her bags and a customs officer set about a professional but laborious inspection more designed to buy them time to run a series of immigration checks than to fulfil any particular fascination with the contents of her designer luggage. When the computer had spat back everything they needed, the men stepped out from behind their barrier and gestured for her to follow them. Her feet remained fixed to the spot and she glanced around for someone—anyone—to come to her aid. No one did. After a moment, the larger of the two men returned the few paces to her side and gestured, not unkindly, towards the interview room.

Perhaps it was the 'please' that Brad saw on his lips in English that got her feet moving. Or perhaps it was the intractable hand at her back that stopped short of actually touching her. Either way the official achieved his aim, and Seraphina Blaise took the first careful steps behind one official while the second flanked her from behind. Just before they left the arrivals area, the man to the rear glanced his way and jerked his head just once in permission.

Brad moved immediately.

Two was bad enough, now there were three. As dark and neutral as the other officials but this one wasn't in the traditional robe and headdress of his people. He looked more like a dark-suited chauffeur. Or a CIA agent. Or a chauffeur for the CIA.

All three men stood on the other side of the soundproof glass of her containment room talking *about* her but not *to* her. The immaculately dressed officials listened attentively—one of them even smiled, which had to be a good sign except that he followed it up with a firm and distinctly suspicious glare in her direction. The chauffeur talked some more, his hands gesticulating wildly.

'Is there a problem?' she asked aloud, with more confidence than she felt, counting on the soundproofing being one-way. Only the chauffeur bothered to look up for the briefest glance before his attention returned to the airport officials and their intense conversation.

This wasn't her first run-in with authorities, but it was her first in such a conservative country where everything was done so differently from Britain. Still, the basic rule applied here as it did everywhere in life…

Show no fear.

But do it politely.

'Perhaps we could please begin?' she called out carefully, as though the only part of this bothering her were the delay. 'I have a service waiting to collect me.'

She threw in a winning smile for good measure. Hopefully, it would temper the *thump-thump* of her heart clearly audible in her voice. But the smile was wasted as the rapid, under-their-breath discussion continued without her. Then the largest of the officials shook the chauffeur's hand and crossed to the table where her documents lay spread out. He flipped her passport open and stamped it with the visa, then initialled it and passed it to him.

She jumped as the glass between the spaces suddenly snapped to opaque, then again a moment later, when the door to her half of the room was flung open and the chauffeur stood there, her bag in one fist and her documentation clenched in the other.

'Welcome to Umm Khoreem,' he said, with no other explanation or apology, wedging the door open.

He might have shared the same tan skin and dark hair as the other officials, but his accent wasn't Arabic. She stared at him, her feet still nailed to the floor as he spelled it out in clearer terms.

'You are free to leave.'

'That's it?' Her passion for natural justice started to bubble. 'Why was I detained in the first place?'

She had a fairly good idea—those few hours in a disguised medical research lab north of London were going to shadow her forever—but she just wanted to hear him say it. Plus, she wanted to narrow down his accent. But he wasn't in the chatty mood, it seemed; he slid his sunglasses on, turned and walked away from her with her suitcase. And her passport.

She hurried after him. 'Can I please have my—?'

'Keep walking, Ms Blaise,' he gritted, nodding towards the distant glass exit. 'You're not legally in the country until we get past that door up ahead.'

His tortured vowels gave her an answer—Australian—and the way he practically barked at her made her reassess him as airport security or some kind of translator. The other officials might have been obstructing her entrance but they were nothing but painfully and professionally courteous. He might have facilitated her release but he was curt and grumpy.

So, if he wasn't airport staff then who was he? Why should she follow a random stranger down some long dark corridor?

Though she had little choice as he marched off with all her worldly goods.

'Sorry, what just happened?' she puffed, hurrying up beside him as he strode along the passageway. Other than, clearly, she was almost refused an entry visa. 'Why did they let me go, just like that?'

He didn't deign to do more than angle his head slightly back as he answered. He certainly didn't stop or even slow. 'They had little option when the ruling Sheikh vouched for you.'

Her feet stumbled to a halt. 'You're a sheikh?'

His laugh ricocheted off the polished walls of the corridor. 'Do I look like a sheikh?'

How would she know? Maybe they were all neat-bearded, square-jawed types. 'Then how—?'

'Sheikh Bakhsh Shakoor is my employer. I therefore spoke on his behalf.'

Oh, everything was starting to make more sense now. 'And why exactly does Sheikh Whatsit care what happens to me?'

Or even know about it, come to think of it? It all happened so quickly. One minute she was happily arriving, the next she was unhappily interned.

'You are a long-stay guest in his most prestigious resort. He would not be pleased to hear you had been detained on a technicality.'

A criminal charge wasn't exactly nothing. That was why she'd declared it on her immigration form. Transparency and accountability and all that. But she was spending a fortune on her month at the Sheikh's desert resort and being booted out of his country bound in red tape would obviously be an expensive outcome for the resort. And since he probably also owned the airport…

'He has no idea what you just did, does he?' she guessed.

'The Sheikh does not have time for trivialities.'

Way to make a girl feel special… 'So, you just got creative?'

His lips pressed closer together as he lifted her suitcase as though it were empty of designer contents and pushed it ahead of them through the official exit into the Umm Khoreem side of the airport.

To freedom.

Kind of.

'I gave them a few assurances,' he went on. 'Nothing that should put a crimp in your sunbaking plans.'

Yep, he probably did think she'd come to bask under Umm Khoreem's toasty winter sun. Rather than for the sanctuary—from life and from her least favourite time of year.

'What kind of assurances?'

The pace he set across the polished stone of the airport terminal was almost hard to match, though it was fantastic to be moving her limbs again after nine hours on a crowded plane. She hurried after him as he wove in and out of the thick stream of passengers like a rally pro.

'While you are within the fenced bounds of Al Saqr resort, you are a guest of the Sheikh,' he said, back to her, 'and his protection extends to you. Under those conditions they were happy to overlook your recent...crime...and grant you entry into Umm Khoreem.'

'You make it sound like I was caught robbing a bank,' she huffed.

'You'd be surprised how much I know about you, Ms Blaise.'

She glanced up at him and tried to guess how serious he was about that. There wasn't much to know. Her criminal record was empty of anything but a shiny new conviction for trespass. For defending those who could not defend themselves.

On balance, that was a pretty good trade-off.

'Wow. Someone is a little judgey...'

It was all there in the frost in his tone and the grind of his jaw, but getting into a fight was not how she'd imagined starting her month-long exile. Then again, neither was being detained, and—once again—she reminded herself how foreign this culture was from her own.

'The resort's boundaries are massive,' he said. 'As long as you remain within them, you'll be fine.'

Being managed irked her as much as it always did. 'And what is to stop me from just taking my bag and disappearing into the glass and chrome of Kafr Falaj?'

She could see the tallest of the capital's buildings from here.

His locomotive surge across the terminal came to an abrupt halt, and she almost crashed into him. Impenetrable black glass swung her way.

'I am.'

Even without being able to see his eyes, she believed him. Her long legs might get her some distance in the short term but his hard build said he would easily best her on endurance. Plus she'd never been any good at running in sand.

'I gave them my own word, too,' he went on.

'So, now I'm beholden to the Sheikh's chauffeur as much as the Sheikh himself?' she tested.

Coral lips thinned between the neatly trimmed

beard and moustache. 'I am not a chauffeur, Ms Blaise. I'm part of the royal protection detail.'

Was she supposed to be impressed that his title had the word 'royal' in it? Well, *snap*, *buddy*, she was celebrity royalty, and it had never done her any particular favours. Quite the opposite, really.

'Which makes me *your* protection detail for the next month,' he added blandly.

Immediately she regretted everything about the past fifteen minutes. It wasn't this guy's fault that she'd been dumb enough to be taken in by people she'd thought she could trust—a *man* she'd wanted to trust—or that it had all happened right before Christmas, a season she struggled with at the best of times. A forty-minute drive was one thing; the thought of spending the next *four weeks* butting heads with someone over baggage that wasn't rightfully his did not appeal. She'd come out here to lie low—and to do the right thing by her father—not to stir up the locals.

But she was more proficient in nurturing chasms than bridging them.

'Gosh, you drew the short straw,' she joked. 'Babysitting *me* for an entire month.'

She'd meant that to be self-deprecating, but she saw the word 'babysit' hit him as surely as the word 'chauffeur' had. His jaw clamped that tiny bit harder.

'On the contrary,' he gritted. 'I drew anything but a short straw. You'll understand when you see where I get to spend the next four weeks.'

She might be known for her questionable decision-making now and again but even she knew to back away from the edge, sometimes. And the stiff way that this man held his body told her that this was definitely one of those times. But retreating didn't mean she had to scramble, so she took her time setting off as he headed for the airport's exit and she swanned after him with as much grace as she could muster, even as the glass doors slid wide and the warm desert air slapped her full in the face.

Outside the window of Al Saqr's luxury SUV the region's capital, Kafr Falaj, whizzed past in all its expensive glory—a spectacular city that had sprung up out of the sand in just a couple of decades. A testament to man's supremacy over nature.

Except that Sera preferred nature's supremacy to mankind's any day.

The travel website had told her it translated as

'*village of channels*', grown on the strength of the massive network of ancient irrigation conduits that rivalled the Roman aqueducts and that still funnelled water from underground aquifers and mountain foothills to the desert village's thriving agriculture. A village that had quickly grown into a city. Thankfully, this was as close as she needed to get to Kafr Falaj and its over-abundance of foreigners—living there, working there, visiting there. Where they were headed, the handful of foreigners would be vastly spread out.

Studying the city had killed some time, then the emerging desert, and, in between, she'd studied *him* while he'd concentrated on the fast desert highway. The neat cut of his dark hair, the crisp edges of his suit collar, the clip of his dark beard so close it had to be a professional job, the curious scar cutting down into his left eyebrow. He hadn't spoken since bundling her into the back seat of the massive SUV. She'd squeezed herself through the gap and into the front passenger seat before he'd even come around to his own door.

She hated the whole Miss Daisy thing. She never rode in the back if she didn't have to.

'So, we're going to spend four weeks in each other's company,' Sera said, simply to crack the long silence as they drove out of the city. 'What should I call you?'

'What did you call your last protection?' he finally grunted.

'Russell it is, then,' she said, smiling. 'What are the odds?'

Dark sunglasses turned her way, just slightly. 'You can call me Brad, Ms Blaise.'

'You know that Blaise is a stage name, right? First and last name all in one. Like Madonna. Or Bono. Apparently that was a thing in the eighties.'

'I assumed.'

But maybe he remembered the vast quantities of money that she was spending on this trip, because he spoke again and this time it was longer than three syllables. 'Would you prefer a different surname?'

'I'd prefer no surname at all, actually.' Ha! Like father like daughter.

'Okay. Seraphina.'

'God no! That's as much of a show name as Blaise. Pretty sure Dad's publicist picked it.' Forgetting that a little girl needed to live with it.

His lips pressed more tightly together within the architectural facial hair. 'What do you call yourself?'

'Sera.'

'Fine. How about we set some ground rules, Sera?'

She'd had a gutful of alpha-male types. They could tie her in knots way too easily. 'You know... you sure are shovey about how things need to be.'

'Establishing parameters is necessary. I have a job to do.'

She opened the console fridge between them in the back seat and cracked the lid on one of several frosty bottles of water she found there. 'I'm not sure how parameters are going to go with me. Didn't you read my file? There must have been a note.'

From her father. Or Russell. Or the security detail before him. Her tutor before that. Any of her nannies. How far back did he want to go?

'There were quite a number of notes, in fact.'

And he struck her as a man who would have read them all. 'I do like to think of myself as noteworthy.'

Again, no reaction to speak of. Just that steady, impermeable, infuriating, Polaroid regard pointed firmly at the road ahead.

'How about I set the first parameter, Brad?' she went on.

'Go ahead.'

'What say whenever any one of us has something to say to the other we remove our sunglasses and make actual eye contact? Like polite people.' She sweetened it with a smile.

Oh, well...start as you mean to continue.

The silence grew weighted—blue whale kind of weighted—but then Brad lowered his head just slightly, removed his glasses and folded them carefully into his breast pocket with the hand not steering, then turned back to meet her eyes square on. But his weren't contrite, and the act didn't weaken him. His regard burned into her as if he were scanning her DNA and, for just a moment, she wished she'd kept her big mouth shut.

Pale grey eyes—combined with his dark colouring they were stunning.

Yep, you're going to need to leave those glasses on...

'You do realise you're textbook, I suppose?' he said as he returned his focus to the traffic around them and she was able to breathe a little easier.

'Textbook what?'

'New client. Trying to control things.'

She glanced out at the eight lanes of pristine highway cutting south through the open desert on the outskirts of the city and thought about making light of it. But then something about the unfairness of his judgement pushed a few of her natural justice buttons.

'Listen, Brad, I've lived my whole life in the care of professional people. A couple of jerks, most of them nice. Some of them completely lovely. But all of *them* were paid to be there, too. I don't think it's too much to ask for a little eye contact when we speak. Just so I know you're real.'

He focused his grey gaze on the highway ahead—thinking, driving—until finally he came to some kind of conclusion. He swung his regard her way again, and a little puff of heat formed at her collar.

'Parameter one,' he agreed on a single nod before turning back to the road. 'Courtesy in all its forms.'

Meaning...?

But, before she could finish the thought, he barrelled onwards while he changed lanes to tuck their black SUV in behind a huge silver one.

'Parameter two,' he continued mildly. 'I'll respect your right to independence if you'll respect my responsibilities as your specialist security detail.'

And if his responsibilities and her rights failed to align…? 'Is that your way of asking me to do whatever you say?'

'It's my way of asking you not to fight me just for the sake of it.'

Hmm. Maybe he *had* read her file.

'Fair enough. Parameter three…' Time to really lay down the law. 'I'm your responsibility, but not your friend. You get to be annoyed but not disappointed if things don't go how you'd like them to.'

Okay, so maybe that baggage wasn't really his to be encumbered with but it couldn't hurt to knock it on the head nice and early. The last thing she needed on her big desert time out was anything that reminded her of her father's not-so-quiet disappointment.

'I'm good with that. Very good, in fact. I'm not here for the conversation.'

She sat back straighter against the plush leather seat. 'Any final comments?'

He considered. 'Parameter four. If you need help—if you really need it—you come to me. No matter what else has gone down between now and then. I'll manage whatever it is.'

There was that word again…

She'd been *managed* her whole life.

'You really have a thing for control, don't you?' Which was tantamount to waving a red tea towel at the bull of her capricious nature.

He shrugged. 'I'm paid to control our environment.'

Her environment, for the next four weeks.

'Okay...' Four weeks was a long time, she needed to lighten things up a bit. 'Courtesy, cooperation, respect and emergency protocol. I think we've covered everything. Except maybe a safe word? I vote for "capsicum".'

His dark brows folded. 'Capsicum?'

'You know...in case either of us needs out of this arrangement at any time?'

If she thought the muscles of his face capable of it, she would have pegged that tiny twist on the right of his mouth as a smile. Probably just gas. Except then he really blew her mind by making a joke.

Kind of.

'What if you're ordering at a restaurant and you say it?' he queried, eyes fixed on the road ahead.

Her perception of him shifted just a little. In an upward direction.

'I'll call them peppers.'

'And if you're planting a garden?'

She matched his straight face. 'In the deserts of Umm Khoreem?'

'What if you're picking out wall colours?'

She laid her hand on her heart. 'I pledge to do no interior decorating until this month is up.'

His eyes returned to hers and—miracle of miracles—they were just a hint warmer than before. More *bark of oak* and less *Thames in winter*.

'Okay.' He nodded. 'Capsicum it is.'

Why did it feel good to have had a small win over this man, even in jest? And exactly when had it started feeling a little bit like flirting?

CHAPTER TWO

THE MORE SHE SPOKE, the more comfortable Brad felt about the month ahead. This wasn't some helpless princess who would flap her hands every time something didn't go her way. She wasn't the needy type. She might well end up being a pain in his butt but at least she wouldn't be looking to him for any kind of rescue. As far as he could see, this gig was more about protecting her from herself.

Still, she was celebrity offspring and he was a pro and so, out of habit, his eyes scanned the many expensive vehicles keeping pace with them at two hundred clicks on the highway away from Kafr Falaj. Each one with extra dark window tinting that obscured its occupants. Once, that would have made him twitchy, but this was Umm Khoreem— there was an oil-rich sea between here and any of the conflict hotspots he'd ever been stationed. And he was here keeping an eye on some rock star's kid, not enforcing sanctions or protecting UN personnel.

Those days were behind him.

He cracked his knuckles and slid his eyes back to his client. Sera had made quite a meal of studying the endless desert since the whole ground-rules conversation had limped to a civil halt between them, and her eyes were still fixed on the massive dunes in the distance as they sped along the Al Dhinn highway.

His mind flashed up the client sheet that her London-based security firm had provided.

Seraphina Blaise. Twenty-four years old, daughter of a middle-aged Goth frontman who'd been performing live for most of Brad's own youth and still was today. A punishing and relentless schedule that kept his band, The Ravens, at the top of the charts whenever they released anything. Blaise didn't really seem old enough to have an adult daughter, but who knew with these rock types— they started their careers young, or made their mistakes early. Whichever.

His daughter's file was full of labels like 'ardent' and 'rash' but also 'committed' and 'loyal'. And 'damaged'. There were screenshots about her very public arrest earlier in the year mixed amongst older citations for volunteering, academic excellence and her talent as a photographer. So which was true? He had citations—a drawer full of them—and they didn't necessarily make him a better person.

Maybe he'd be better off ignoring what was in Sera's file and conducting his own assessment.

Her tongue might be a little sharp but it worked for a pretty switched-on brain; not everyone called him out as thoroughly as she had just now. It was hard not to respect a pre-emptive striker even if she was overly cranky. She'd just been detained by one of the toughest and touchiest governments in the world—he'd throw her a bone on that one.

She'd been carved by some kind of post-modern sculptor. A whole bunch of mismatched parts that came together into an intriguingly curious package. Everything about her was long. Her face, her jaw, her nose. Hair. Fingers. Legs. It reminded him of Al Saqr's best Arab horses but still managed to be feminine. It shouldn't really work together but somehow it did, leaving her more... striking than classically pretty. She didn't accessorise with copious amounts of jewellery the way most of her flight had; other than the silver clasps on her flimsy blouse, the treacle-brown hair tumbling down over her bare shoulders was all the decoration she needed.

On the other hand, she'd swanned into a conservative country with her arms and shoulders bare. Ordinarily, he would have chalked that up to cultural ignorance, but in Sera... He found it hard to imagine that she hadn't read up on the region she was visiting. It was almost as if she was challenging Umm Khoreem to a silent social debate.

Maybe she was. Her file was full of protests and causes and righteous indignation about one thing or another.

For the second time in forty minutes, Brad hit the indicator to change lanes, and he navigated the SUV around and under the highway to reach the start of Al Saqr's access road. He let the massive vehicle own the road; when the resort was as exclusive and private as Al Saqr, oncoming traffic was rarely an issue.

Sera sat up straighter to see what was ahead. The composed woman he'd seen at the airport was morphing, with every stretch of her long neck, into a different creature. A more excited, engaged, relaxed woman.

Or maybe the desert was just wielding its subtle magic already. It was good like that.

'Still fifteen minutes,' Brad murmured, and she slumped back into her seat like an impatient teen.

He forced himself not to smile. 'Is this your first desert?'

'Not counting ones I've flown over? Yes.'

'Whatever you're expecting,' he murmured, 'you're wrong.'

Her eyebrows raised, but she didn't bite. She peered, instead, out the front of the vehicle at the vast…nothing…that was ahead of them.

Five minutes later, he pulled to a halt at Al Saqr's armed boundary checkpoint. Per the regulations, the guard came out and eyeballed the whole vehicle—including the empty back seats—checking Sera's name off the sparse guest register before waving them through the raised boom gate. In his periphery, Sera eyed the massive mesh fences stretching out in both directions as far as she could see and the casual way the guard's high-powered weapon was slung over his shoulder. For the first time, her confidence seemed to wobble. Just a little.

'Do you get much trouble out here?'

'The fences are to protect the wildlife,' he reassured. Though, in truth, they went a long way to making his job easier given the only people allowed past Al Saqr's checkpoint were registered guests, staff and suppliers. That lessened his field of professional concern from everyone on the Arabian Peninsula to just a comparative handful.

Although something told him that Sera, herself, would be dominating his field of concern for the next few weeks of his life.

That elegant neck started craning again as they left the asphalt and hit the compacted road gouged through the desert. Around them, the geometric shapes carved by wind into the sand and the occasional fire bush dominated. But as they crested a high dune she got her first glimpse of the resort far ahead, nestled in the middle of an enormous expanse of interlocking, golden blonde sand dunes.

Like the oasis it functionally was.

'It's gorgeous,' Sera breathed.

Yeah, it was. The resort stretched like a jewelled tiara along the top edge of a massive sand ridge.

Not that the desert needed any gilding.

The date palms that signalled the presence of shallow groundwater started to whizz by, first in singles, then in spikey clusters. Tucked away between small dune rises on their left and right were small, scattered buildings—service sites for the resort and their staff—but the road kept on moving past those, disappointing Sera visibly every time one was not part of the larger resort. Finally, the palm clusters merged into a proper croft and Sidr and Ghaf trees thickened up around them as neat herringbone pavers seemed to emerge from the graded sand like the yellow brick road in Oz.

Just as well, too, or Sera would have run out of seat to climb. He glanced sideways at her and tried hard not to acknowledge that curiosity did good things to her face.

'Oh, wow!'

He loved this part. The moment that someone saw Al Saqr for the first time. The luxury resort that she would be calling home for the next month.

He scanned the arrivals area ahead as they pulled into the paved circle in front of the resort's reception despite knowing that no one but authorised personnel and guests could have been inside the fences. Old habits died hard.

'Standby,' he instructed, levering his door handle.

Dry heat rushed past him as he climbed out, still scanning for threats, then crossed quickly in front of the SUV to open the passenger side door as two staff emerged from the heavy timber entrance of the resort's central hub. The shorter of the two was traditionally but comfortably dressed, smiling broadly enough to pop dimples, his hand outstretched. Behind him stood a taller man, ginger haired, dressed in khaki and boots.

They nodded briefly to Brad then stood at attention as he gave Sera his arm down from the high SUV.

She stepped forward enthusiastically as soon as her feet touched earth.

'Hi!'

Brad closed the SUV door quietly and stood in much the same pose as his colleagues—hands behind him, back straight—as they introduced themselves to Sera. There was little sign of the woman from the airport, now. This Sera had pulled her thick hair back in a desert-friendly ponytail while she was waiting for him to clear the arrivals area and wore undisguised excitement on her face. You had to be a real tough guy to remain unaffected by Al Saqr's unique beauty.

This Sera was more girl than woman, and the unfamiliar twist in his gut hit him again.

'Ms Blaise, welcome,' the shorter of the two men said in impeccable English, pressing an introduction card into her hand for her later reference. 'I am Aqil, your guest relations coordinator. Anything you need, do not hesitate to ask for me.'

Eric was taller, and he leaned around Aqil to

shake Sera's hand and introduce himself before adding, 'I'm an Al Saqr field guide. You'll be doing your activities with me.'

Two more staff emerged with a guest trolley and quietly collected Sera's luggage from the SUV as Aqil and Eric ushered her beyond the main doors. Brad followed the arctic air that pumped out through the opening courtesy of air-conditioning powered by the ocean of solar panels tucked between the dunes out of guest view. No matter how many times he was assigned out here, stepping inside was always like walking into Aladdin's cave. Cool, dark and just a little bit mystic. Traditional Arabian architecture and furnishings had been put to good use in the resort's foyer, and the whole place smelled vaguely...herbal. It had an immediate impact on Sera.

'I wish I'd kept my camera out of my luggage,' she murmured, running her eyes from the labyrinthine floor tiles up to the ornate timber roof features.

Aqil turned a winning smile on her. 'It is beautiful, no? You will be in this building often over the coming weeks. Many opportunities. This way, please.'

They guided her into the receiving lounge off to

one side of the foyer, filled with richly upholstered sofas and low, old tables. Old in a good way—an expensive way—not old like the beaten-up furniture he remembered from his UN days in the desert villages. Eric returned with a tall glass of tropical fruit juice for Sera.

'While you rest here I'll just have a word with your liaisons,' Brad murmured.

She might have heard him, she might not. Her attention was so thoroughly taken by the feel of the woven sheaves hanging over the arched doorway and the intricate wrought iron decorating the window looking back out to the foyer. But he took momentary leave to check in with Aqil and Eric.

Their focus shifted immediately once they were out of Sera's presence.

'What's the protocol?' Aqil said quietly.

'Close contact,' he briefed them, fast. Which meant he needed to be on hand nearby. Very nearby. 'Where have you put her?'

Aqil consulted the site map spread on his desk. 'Suite ten is vacant on both sides.'

Ten was good. Far enough away from other guests for privacy and quiet but close enough to the main buildings for a fast response if needed. And it meant he could set up camp in eleven, right next door. Al Saqr had multi-roomed suites, but an unrelated man and woman under one roof on the Arabian Peninsula…? Nope, not even if she was under serious threat. But better safe than sorry. Celebrity did weird things to people.

And he didn't take any risks these days. He'd come too close in the past.

'No one enters her suite when she's in it unless I'm present,' he ordered.

'Understood.'

He rattled off a few other need-to-knows and then turned back to the lounge where Sera had finished fondling the curtains and sat, happy as a clam, sipping her juice on the luxuriously padded traditional lounge. Her smile was as bright as the desert outside when he returned to her side.

'It's all so amazing,' she gushed.

His gut twisted that little bit more. He didn't want her softening. He didn't want bright innocence to start peeking out from behind the façade. He wanted the self-assured, cranky client to stay. Because she was easier to dislike.

And dislike was easier to manage.

'Ready for your room?'

She glanced longingly at the juice still half-full in her hand then back at him.

He caught the smile before it infected the rest of his neutral expression. 'Those are as common as sand out here.'

She took one final long, hard suck on her straw, then placed the glass down on the carved coaster that had been discreetly laid out for her.

'Let's go.'

Al Saqr must look a bit like a scorpion from the air, Sera thought. Long stretches of treed pathway extended out from the resort's main building like articulated legs, going in different directions along the bank of the massive dune the resort was built on. Dotted along them at private yet accessible distances were the individual suites.

Not rooms exactly, she saw as they passed two that weren't theirs, more like quasi-tents with the same plastered white walls and dark timber windows as the resort, but with canopied canvas roofs sitting like a broad sun hat over each hexagonal suite. With timber deck everywhere its shadows reached.

She sighed as her eyes fell on every new and alien thing. Nothing here would remind her of the media and their scrabbling. Or of home. Or the season.

'Here we are,' Aqil advised, pulling the courtesy buggy into the shade of a suite about halfway along the front leg of the scorpion, facing all that empty desert.

The way the suites were staggered, it was easy to feel that it was just she and the desert. No other human being or work as far as the eye could see. She took her time getting off the buggy, knowing that Brad would get there before her and indeed he did, sweeping inside as soon as the door opened and clearing the room before she was allowed into it. She smiled awkwardly at Aqil, who just shrugged and waited in patient, dimpled silence with her.

Stepping inside was totally worth the wait. Cool and dim and fragrant. Just like the resort reception. But that was where the similarity ended. This was a suite that managed to be simple yet more luxurious than anything she'd ever stayed in before. The six-sided shape of the room was countered by custom furniture in traditional style so that everything fitted without making it feel cluttered. Long sofas, luxury coffee station, writing desk and an opulent, high, king-sized bed centred against it all. Three of the six edges of the suite were glass doors with thick light-controlling drapes of the same kind of silken weave she'd gone crazy patting earlier.

Until Aqil flung one set open.

Beyond the glass doors, the Arabian desert flowed golden and dramatic, its dunes laid out in all their glory all the way to the horizon where the shadows of mountains loomed. And immediately in front, between all that sand and her air-conditioned life-support system, a gorgeous, deep, blue plunge pool, half in desert sun, half in shade.

Sera pressed her hands to the glass doors and leaned into the heat soaking in through them. Hot desert. Cold pool. Espresso station. Massive *Princess and the Pea* bed...

Some of the tension she'd been carrying around for the past year shifted and broke away, turning to dust on the warm desert breeze.

'Your home for the next month,' Aqil murmured. 'Let me show you everything...'

It only took a few minutes, yet there was nothing she could need that Al Saqr hadn't thought of. Lazy luxury from top to bottom.

'Mr Kruger is in the suite immediately to your right,' Aqil said when the tour was done, handing Brad an old-fashioned, hand-wrought key that matched hers. 'His bag has been placed there already.'

On cue, hers was whisked in. Even with only one bag, she'd over-packed. Right now she would be entirely happy to spend the whole month in her swimsuit, though probably she'd need to throw on a dress to go for food now and then. She glanced at the table set up by the pool.

Unless she had dinner come to her...

Another knot in her shoulder unravelled.

'Aqil, thank you. This is...exactly what I needed.'

Silence. Beauty. Nature. Far enough from civilisation that even *she* couldn't cause a stir out here. The perfect place to lie low for a bit.

And not a hint of Christmas festivity.

'We pride ourselves on being what our guests need, Miss Blaise,' Aqil murmured. Then he excused himself, told her how she could contact him if she needed him and departed. She leaned back on the warm glass doors, closed her eyes and let even more of the tension soak away into that heat.

When they reopened, Brad was still there. Waiting quietly for instructions.

Kruger. Brad Kruger. A strong name for a strong man.

'I'm going to dig out my camera,' she said, pushing the thought away as firmly as she pushed herself away from the glass. 'And I'm going to take a swim. And lie on this day lounge. Possibly not in that order. Why don't you get settled in next door and come back when you're done? We can talk about how this is all going to work.'

He nodded—the only discernible part of his inscrutable expression—and departed, leaving just her, her heavy heart and the non-judgemental desert.

Brad tore himself away from the familiar view and got up off the sofa. Getting 'settled' had only taken him a few minutes—how long could it take to unpack one small bag and lay out basic toiletries in the obscenely large bathroom?

If Sera's UK security were paying for anything other than close contact then he would be back in his own apartment in the city, driving out to the resort every morning to supervise his client. But close contact meant *close* and so he'd be enjoying the resort's six-star facilities gratis for the next month. His eyes strayed back out to the soft, rich light falling onto the desert sands.

There were definitely worse ways to spend your Christmas.

He'd heard the distant splash of Sera lowering herself into her pool a while earlier, so he trusted that she was too busy enjoying the view to be getting up to any early mischief. But he'd figured she could probably use a little mental space after her dramatic arrival in the country, so he'd cooled his heels for the twenty minutes after unpacking, then done a token perimeter assessment of both their suites to stretch it out a little more.

In his experience, protec*tees* never adjusted quite as well to the idea of close contact as the protec*tors*, even the ones whose lives depended on high-level guard. It was a skill, hitting that fine balance between too much and too little supervision. Relaxed enough to keep your client sane and compliant, but not so relaxed that it opened a window for the kind of risk that he was hired to protect them against. And not so much that the client became overly reliant on you and stopped listening to their own instincts. Overly reliant or overly fond—the small twist in his gut reminded him. That was just as dangerous. As he'd discovered the hard way.

The best balance was...indifferent acquiescence.

That was what he'd be pushing for with Sera.

His suite, which also meant hers, was unchanged from the last time he was assigned to Al Saqr—

locked from the inside, glass doors on three sides, huge pair of timber doors on the public side, privacy fences all around but open to desert everywhere else. Rule of thumb here was that you kept your desert walks away from your neighbouring accommodations; a privacy thing. So staff wouldn't visit while Sera was in the suite and no one should be hauling themselves up the dune face and stumbling into her private pool area any time soon.

Though *shouldn't* and *wouldn't* weren't necessarily the same thing. His formal orders were to make sure Sera stayed out of trouble while the media attention from her recent legal troubles died down, but when your father was as rich and famous as hers, anything was possible. And he wasn't about to get caught out by letting his guard down.

Once burned, ten times shy.

Brad locked suite eleven's door behind him and jogged past Sera's to the neighbours on the other side to confirm nine was definitely empty. Then he checked his watch to ensure a full hour had passed and he presented himself back at her door, knocking firmly.

He counted to ten before trying again.

Still nothing.

'Sera?'

His chest filled with lead. *Please don't let her have gone exploring alone…*

Just because she'd agreed to ground rule number two in the SUV didn't mean she'd stick to it when faced with the seductions of this unique place. He stepped down off the decking leading to the front door and walked around the side of the suite where his own had a side opening for maintenance staff to use. He could hear a bunch of animal noises he didn't recognise—one of them a kind of gaspy hitch—so the wildlife around them could be just about anything.

'Sera?' Something about the desert silence made him not want to shout. 'I'm coming around.'

But as he stepped back up on to the decking within her back yard, his quick eyes saw exactly why Sera hadn't heard him. She floated at the deep end of her little pool, the water cascading over her arms that lay folded on its tiled infinity edge, chin resting there, staring out at the desert beyond. Her long hair looked even darker wet and it hung flat down her back between pale shoulders and blue swimsuit straps, which made it easy to see the headphones she had wedged into her ears. He followed the white wires over to where her phone rested on the flat, dry tiles of the pool edge.

Something about her posture stilled his feet before he reached the steps, though.

And then he heard it… The choked hitch he'd attributed in amongst the other desert wildlife sounds. It wasn't an exotic bird calling at all; it was Sera, crying—sobbing, actually, if only she weren't doing such a good job of muffling it in her folded arms. He stood, frozen, and stared at her heaving shoulders and back. Everything in him burned to go and check on her. The urge bubbled up and made his feet twitch.

But a single image fought its way through all the instinct and kept him utterly immobile—a young, glittery-eyed face, splotched red with distress, pressed up against the rear window of a hastily departing transporter, his little mouth open in a cry that Brad couldn't hear.

But he'd felt it down to his very soul.

He still did.

Sera's tears could be about just about anything. The ex-boyfriend her file said she'd parted ways with. Bad news from home. Work hassles, if not for the fact that she didn't have a job, at least, not a proper one. Her father's money had brought her freedom from the worries of ordinary people.

He stared at the soft lurches of her pale shoulders.

Clearly, money hadn't exactly bought her happiness.

Whatever it was, it wasn't any of his business until it put her at physical risk. His job was to keep Sera out of trouble for four weeks. Muddling around in her emotional well-being was completely outside his remit. He wasn't paid for it.

And he wasn't remotely skilled at it.

He took a backwards step, and then another, and vanished the way he'd come, leaving Sera to her privacy.

And her pain.

CHAPTER THREE

'HAVE YOU TASTED the bananas?' Sera burst out, answering his door knock a little later. 'They're amazing. God, I've missed bananas.'

Brad reeled a little at the sheer joy on her face. Quarter of an hour ago she was inconsolable. Maybe the desert with its ever-changing moods was a fitting place for her.

'Is there some kind of British banana shortage I'm not aware of?' he said, rather than obsess on things that were outside his purview.

She turned and walked back into her suite, leaving him to follow. 'I stopped eating them. All our bananas are flash-frosted and shipped in from West Africa or South America; it's been ages since I've had a fresh, locally harvested banana. Sensational.'

Somehow, she'd even managed to make fruit political.

'Are you okay?'

She smiled, and it appeared totally sincere. Obviously a quick rebounder, then.

'Sure. Are you?'

He narrowed his focus on her red-tinged eyes. 'Do you need some eye drops?'

Really, Kruger? You gotta keep snooping? Let it go, man.

She waved his concern away. 'The pool is lightly salted.'

A little bit extra now, given her copious tears. But her easy dismissal made it impossible for him to exercise the absurd Galahad complex she seemed to have triggered in him.

Seraphina Blaise did not need—or want—his help.

His attention tracked to her still-unpacked luggage. 'How are you settling in?'

Her mouth split into a smile as wide as the desert they sat in. 'It's unbelievable, already. Have you seen the light? It changes by the hour. It's going to be amazing to photograph.'

'We'll be doing a bit of that, then?'

'I'm here for a month,' she murmured. 'I'll go mad without a focus. Besides, it's what I *do*. You know?'

Yeah. He knew all about her photography. It was

what had got her in the papers in the first place. Taking photos of animals in confidential research labs. And getting caught doing it. Though that hadn't been quite the accident she'd first believed.

'I figure I'll be busiest in the mornings and late afternoon, when it's coolest and the light is richest,' she said. 'Do you…? Are you supposed to be twenty-four-seven?'

The settling-in phase was always clunky, but Sera managed to make it feel extra awkward. As if he were some kind of stalker and they were negotiating the terms on which he'd lurk around after her.

'I'll be seven days a week for the next month,' he confirmed. 'But I won't be in your face all the time.'

'There'll probably be three or four hours in the hottest part of the day when I'll retreat in here. That's time off for you.'

'Maybe,' he hinted. It all depended on what she got up to while she was alone. Complementary WiFi was a potentially dangerous thing. All it would take was one culturally bolshie blog…

'I'm your protection, Sera. My job is to be here when and if something happens.' And *something* could whip up like a sandstorm. 'I'm not going to be out having shots at the bar when you might need me.'

She stared him down and it reminded him much more of Sera from the airport. 'This place is like Fort Knox. What could possibly happen to me here?'

Any question whether or not she knew what he was truly here for evaporated on the warm desert air.

Okay, time to toss his cards on the table...

'My brief is to ensure you keep a low profile for the next month,' he admitted.

'Actually, that's my brief,' Sera said. '*You're* here because my father clearly doubts my ability to honour my promise to him.'

The politics of her family had no more place in his mind than her tears did. Nor the confused hurt that had just flashed across her bold gaze. He forced his natural empathy aside.

'Your UK security firm are taking no chances,' he said. 'I'm paid for close contact, which means twenty-four-seven.' Or as much as the culture here would allow. 'That will keep you safe from any crazies and—conveniently—means I'll be around to head off any...social issues that might emerge.'

'What if I pledge not to publish any manifestos while I'm here?' she joked.

He couldn't match her light laugh. That was exactly the sort of thing he was hired to restrict. 'I'll be resetting your device passwords daily. More often if I need to.'

'Of course you will,' she grunted. 'Why not just take them off me?'

'Because you're not a child.'

The irony of that made her laugh. 'Thanks for noticing.'

'My job is to create an environment that limits risk, Sera. I'm your protection, not your parent. You already have one of those.'

Again, the flash across her gaze. But while her irritation was real it didn't seem directed at him.

'You can't work around the clock, Brad,' she said, and he got the sense that the idea was genuinely troubling her.

'You'll barely know I'm—'

'I'm not worried for me,' she interrupted. 'It's not fair on you. I'm sorry that you have to be inconvenienced for something that won't even be happening. I had hoped that no one would be put out by me this Christmas,' she muttered.

Was it his imagination or was there an extra

subtle leaning on the word '*this*'? But curiosity belonged between them about as much as empathy did.

Indifferent acquiescence...

'It's not an inconvenience. It's my job. Besides, personal protection isn't exactly taxing,' he said.

'Until it is?' she guessed.

Again, that sharp mind at work.

'Nature of the beast,' he murmured. 'It's all waiting around and watching until it blows up.'

'Well, it won't be blowing up because of me,' she vowed with determination in her eyes. 'No matter what my father thinks. I'm afraid it's going to be a dull month for you.'

Yeah... The road to hell was paved with good intentions. 'Did your last protection detail buy that gentle sincerity?'

Right before he got reassigned over the whole research-lab debacle.

He deserved her annoyance, but the flush he got instead was shame. It peaked high in her cheeks and cast her eyes downward.

'I'll be all right,' he assured her in lieu of apology. 'I'll take my downtime as I can.'

'I just want you to know that I'm okay with the idea of personal space,' she murmured.

He couldn't help the laugh then. 'I'm sure. Unfortunately, I'm required to intrude on yours quite a bit.'

She sighed and moved to the bedside table to collect her key. 'Well, we might as well get on with it, then. The resort schedules a complimentary spa session for anyone who has come in on an international flight. Mine's in half an hour.'

Back on the job. 'I'll call up the buggy.'

'I'd like to walk. To get some pictures before the spa,' she said. 'Then perhaps some more shooting after lunch.'

It wasn't a request, no matter how politely delivered. Here was a woman who'd been negotiating with protection details her whole life, though, while she was good at it, her tension told him she didn't enjoy it. Fortunately, he did. Clear, confident directions boded well for a client who would accept his daily intrusions into her life.

'Sounds good,' he said.

In reality, protection details were dull more often than they were *good*. The trick was in staying alert and on your game while your mind turned to mush watching some client reading a book or watching their kid at a ball game or catching a movie. The consequences of losing focus could be bad. And prevention was a whole lot better than cure.

As he knew from experience.

Sera grabbed her camera from her luggage and a wide straw hat from her bedhead and turned for the door.

'Let's go.'

'Did the floor say something to offend?' Sera asked him, her voice husky from an hour of languorous spoiling in the spa. The rest of her was buried in her oversized robe, enjoying the dazed, spaced-out, post-massage moments.

Brad's grey gaze shot upwards as he pushed to his feet. 'Sorry, what?'

Her smile was as slow to form as her slurred words, but the uncomfortable expression on his face as he looked her over made her want to double-check that the robe was closed everywhere it should be. It made her want to fix her just-massaged hair, too, but she resisted the urge.

'The floor,' she clarified. 'You're frowning at it pretty severely.'

'We, uh, disagreed on a few fundamentals.'

His gruff chuckle did more for undoing the stresses of her arrival in Umm Khoreem than the hour-long rubdown she'd just enjoyed. Or the good, cathartic cry she'd had in the pool. A laugh, on this man, was as surprising and rare as the light out here.

'Feel good?' he said, dragging himself up into professional guard stance.

'Amazing.' She smiled.

Her new favourite word. The desert was amazing. The suites were amazing. The massages were amazing. For someone who so easily found the beauty in the visual, her grasp of the verbal was taking a real hit this trip. It had to be connected to those eyes.

She never should have ordered him to take his sunglasses off.

'I'll wait by the door,' Brad said, nudging her towards the changing room. She stumbled forward in her half-drugged state.

The Sera that emerged from the change rooms fifteen minutes later was more the woman she liked to present to the world. She'd taken her time redressing and scrunching her hair into something vaguely stylish—using every complimentary product in the place and delighting in the complex, Arabian smells—and her bare arms and throat practically glistened from whatever oils her masseuse had used on her. She felt spoiled and mellow and fresh.

She signed her tab at the spa's reception desk and then turned and floated out the door. Brad trailed behind her, playing Sherpa to her camera gear.

'Don't forget to eat,' he murmured. 'One banana isn't going to keep you going for long, no matter how delicious it was.'

'After that massage I'm ravenous. Let's go get lunch,' she said. Sometimes—just sometimes—it was nice to have someone to do your thinking for you.

They headed for the resort's pretty hub, stopping only once to take a photograph along the way—a leggy young gazelle standing in the sand, its little tail waggling madly. Sera captured its markings, coat colour and the deep, watery depths of its eyes. Then she remembered her growly stomach.

Brad had ditched the suit in favour of dark jeans and a light shirt, but he'd kept the pricey glasses firmly in place and added a neutral baseball cap for good measure. Totally Secret Service now. Did he imagine he blended right in with the other guests? Given how he carried himself, he probably blended in nowhere outside some elite force of Arab mercenaries.

It was all very distracting.

She forced her focus back onto the landscape as they wandered along the winding stone pathway criss-crossed by the traditional watercourse that ran through the whole resort. The light was gorgeous even in the middle of the day—textures, colour—and everywhere she looked were images worthy of capturing later. The wind ripples on a bank of sand that looked otherwise completely solid. Plants she'd never seen. Birds she'd never seen. A crazy little side-winding lizard that took its twisty time cutting across in front of her.

But right now she was all about eating. And partly about ignoring the man tailing so close behind her.

He followed her over the doorway plinth into Al Saqr's heart—literally over it, all doors in the resort were cut into a much larger timber frame to keep the sand out—onto the plush rugs scattered across the stone floor. The heat and glare immediately dropped off. It took a moment for her eyes to adjust but only a moment longer to scan the entire space. The restaurant hanging off the back of the main building offered darkened, delicious-smelling dining indoors, or decorated, shade-covered tables on its deck, peering over the desert water-hole below.

'Outside, I think,' Sera said, when asked for her preference.

A minute later, she was seated on the edge of the deck, looming over the desert, her favourite juice on hand and a jug of icy water delivered. They seated Brad a few tables back, out of her view but presumably where he had a good clear outlook over the whole area. If she were her father, there was no way his security would have let him sit here, so exposed to anyone bedded down in a distant dune. But the kind of obsessive crazies The Ravens' gothic music occasionally attracted and the kind of pathetic try-hards *she* would attract were totally different creatures.

The only shot someone was going to take at *her* would end up in the tabloids, not in a morgue.

There were six other diners also having a late lunch, all of them in couples and looking very loved up. This was exactly the right sort of resort for honeymoons or anniversaries. Or romantic Christmases, as it turned out. On balance, though, it was still better to spend the festive season here than back home. Alone.

Even if she was in disgrace.

Her meal came, and right behind that Brad's did. They each ate in silence, the occasional clink of his cutlery a kind of Morse code reminding her he was close by. Sera never once turned to look at him but his presence almost *hummed*; the silence was thick with it. It dragged her attention off the gorgeous view and the delicious cuisine until she might as well have been eating airline food.

When the staff came to remove her first-course dishes, Sera pushed her chair back, turned and marched towards him.

'This is crazy. Come and join me.'

'I'm on the job,' he declined. 'But thank you.'

'Okay, you've said what your employer would want you to say. Now, please join me.'

His eyes didn't quite meet hers. 'Let's just keep it by the book.'

His manners did little more than irritate her further. Partly because she wasn't getting her way. Mostly because she was supposed to be off men—she shouldn't want his company.

But she did.

'What's problematic about having a conversation while we eat?'

His grey eyes turned wary. 'I'm paid to shadow you, not monopolise you.'

'I don't feel monopolised,' she said, low, glancing around at the other diners. 'I feel conspicuous.'

'You're not used to dining alone?'

Was he kidding? She was mostly alone, even when she had company. A nanny had always eaten with her when she was younger but it was always a very...functional exercise. Any conversation they'd had was mostly limited to which hand she held her fork in or whether she had to eat all of her beans. 'In case it's escaped your notice this is a very *coupley* resort.'

His gaze scanned the pairs dotted around the restaurant. 'You want it to seem like we're together?'

Her hiss of annoyance drew more than one curious look. 'Look. I'm the client, asking you to join me for—' she glanced around for inspiration '—my safety!'

He wasn't the slightest bit moved.

'Okay, forget it. I'll just go back to my gorgeous view and have no one to talk about it with.'

With that, she turned and flounced back to her seat, taking an oversized gulp of her dewy melon juice and sinking lower than before into her padded chair.

Stuff him—she was not about to beg. She'd never begged for someone's company in her life.

No matter how tempted she might have been.

* * *

The first Sera knew that Brad had moved was the scrape of the chair opposite hers. He stepped into the gap he'd created, placed his iced water on the table and sank down in front of her.

'The reason we don't do this,' he said without waiting for any kind of response from her, 'is that it sets up awkwardness later. What if you want to dine alone in future? What if I do? This way there's no pressure or expectation on either side. Everything remains easy.'

She turned a baleful glare at him. 'You think I'm going to *expect* you to dine with me?'

He held his mettle and her gaze. 'You wouldn't be the first female client to misinterpret the terms of service for their protection. The rules exist for a reason.'

'If you can't handle yourself with some cougar, Brad, that's on you.' She turned back out to the desert.

His voice next came quietly—amused but slightly disappointed.

Oh, well...join the queue! Her father had communicated more disappointment in the past few months than any other sentiment all year.

'You didn't strike me as a sulker.'

'I'm not sulking,' she gritted, forcing patience she didn't feel. 'I wanted to... I don't do the reach-out thing, normally.'

Because reaching out just wasn't worth the potential rejection, in her experience. Which begged the question: Why bother, now?

'But?'

'But...even if some newspaper did track me out here into the middle of all this nothing, those gigantic fences and armed guards mean there's no chance of a picture ending up in some tabloid with a fabricated story. I just hoped that maybe I could ease back a bit on the rules this trip. Since no one knows who I am out here. You know, relax.'

His steady regard made her fingers twitch, and she curled them subtly into her fists. It only seemed to drive the flutters inward, just below her sternum.

'No one here knows you,' he said, still without blinking, 'but everyone knows me. These are my colleagues.'

The flutters fell to the floor of her gut and died there. That was right. Her plea for some latitude was essentially asking Brad to compromise his professionalism.

Remorse congealed in her blood.

'Sorry, I wasn't thinking.' Well, she was…but not about him. 'Maybe you should—'

He stopped her before she could send him away.

'Leaving again is going to draw more attention than me staying,' he murmured. 'Let's just finish lunch, yeah?'

But having achieved the company she'd set out to secure, Sera suddenly found herself struggling for a single fascinating thing to say. And he was apparently not about to help her out.

'So, you're ex-military?' she finally guessed, though she wouldn't win any prizes for intuition. Everything about him screamed Defence Forces.

'Ten years in the Specials.'

Ten years? She was just a kid when he was first heading into danger. Was that why she felt so breathless around him? Like some sixteen-year-old? She *was* a mere teen, compared to his life experience. 'You seem to know a fair bit about deserts.'

He paused, his fork halfway to his lips. 'More than most.'

'Were you posted to the Middle East?'

'My unit provided support to the United Nations. Mostly based in the capital. But I got out in the sand often enough.'

That brought her eyes back up. 'That sounds interesting.'

'If by "interesting" you mean political and volatile, sure.'

'When did you leave the UN?'

His eyes darkened over. 'Two years ago, now.'

'What made you leave?'

His eyes flicked out to the horizon.

'A mistake,' he murmured, discomforted. 'My mistake.'

She wanted to quiz him further but every question she posed made her feel like that cougar that he'd mentioned; the rare Snoopy Desert Cougar.

'And you've worked for the Sheikh since then?'

'As soon as the opportunity came up. I held out for his team.'

'Why?'

He shrugged massive shoulders. 'They're the best.'

'Must have been competitive,' she murmured.

'So am I.'

Did he have any idea how intriguing that twisted thing he called a smile was?

'And you're always based out here?'

'Not always. But Al Saqr is the gem in Sheikh

Bakhsh Shakoor's crown. All his guests come here at some point, which makes for pleasant work.'

She leaned back in her seat and smiled. 'How many of *them* couldn't leave again without risking deportation?'

He fought a proper smile, but failed. As with the last glimmer she'd had of it, it transformed his face. 'You have the honour of being the first. *My* first, anyway.'

The idea of being Brad's first *anything* resurrected all those butterflies lying prone in her gut and they lurched back to life. She fought to focus on their conversation.

'Who was your most challenging client?'

'It would be unprofessional of me to comment.'

'No names, obviously.'

He stared in silence. Until she realised.

'Truly,' she gasped. 'I'm your worst?' How few had he had?

'You didn't say worst,' he was quick to reply. 'You said challenging.'

'We've been here three hours. How can I possibly challenge you already?'

For the first time, she got the sense that he wasn't saying exactly what was on his mind. 'Do you think I improvise immigration incidents every day?'

'Well, you didn't seem the slightest bit troubled by it.'

Irritated, yes…

'It's my job to appear in control.'

Seriously? Did he have to remind her every five seconds that he was paid to be here?

A beautifully dressed young woman appeared at their table with two flat stone platters dotted with pretty little desserts. She placed them down with a gentle smile, enquired after their needs and then tiptoed off again. Brad's eyes glanced after her.

For no reason at all that made her grumpy.

'So, are we okay to get some photos this afternoon?' she said, drawing his focus back to her. 'Once it starts to get cooler?'

'Whatever you need.'

He inclined his head, waiting politely for her to lift her dessert fork. She was happy to oblige, tucking into a mysterious, bluish sticky morsel—totally foreign to her but scrumptious—and the next ten minutes were all about eating in silence. Until he broke it.

'What's the story with the photography?' he asked. 'Hobby or job?'

Here we go. He wasn't the first person to assume that someone with money didn't want or need to work.

'I don't know that I've sold enough shots to truthfully call it a job,' she said. 'But I take it much more seriously than a hobby. Maybe we could settle on it being a…pastime?'

'How'd you get into it?' His interest seemed more than just polite.

'I don't remember whose idea it was, but I remember the excitement of the day my tutor took me shopping to buy my first equipment. And Friday afternoons when a professional photographer came out to teach me how to use it with any skill.'

'Do you remember what your first photograph was?'

Did she ever.

'A picture of Blaise. I ended up framing it on the wall.' But not because it was good—which it wasn't—it was so she could see her father every day. 'Then it was endless semi-skilled portraits of the staff who looked after me.'

She'd cheerfully showed them the good ones—hungry for their praise—but it wasn't those images that she'd kept. Instead, she'd papered her room with images of them captured unawares or unprepared; tidying their hair for the real photo or glancing at each other before posing properly. Laughing. Smiling. Pulling a face. Natural. As though her everyday life were simply swimming in such unguarded moments. Photography let her rebuild her world the way she wished it were…instead of how it actually was.

Who'd want to look at an exhibition of images of people carefully keeping their distance?

'Once I photographed my first London stray, though, I was all about animals. And how they intersect in the city environment. That's where I really had the best result. I don't think people are really my thing.' In so many ways. 'That led me to photograph shelter animals, to help get them new homes. I enjoyed that.'

'Not too many strays out here,' he murmured.

She thought about that. 'Stray is merely what we call "wild" in urban areas. Not much of a distinction. And the wildlife has plenty of opportunities to interact with human environments out here.'

Brad studied her close, and seemed to be wrestling with something. Finally he spoke again.

'Can I ask you something else?'

'Depends.' She smiled. 'Will it lead me to bore you to tears about my photography?'

But he didn't smile at her joke. On the contrary,

his face sobered up until it was the professional mask again. 'Is there anything I need to know? About earlier... In the pool?'

Every muscle in her body coiled tighter. She shouldn't be surprised he knew about her big cry-fest. He was trained to know. But how did you tell someone you'd just met that you'd been waiting all year for that cry? That you'd been holding on to the indignity of your arrest and the disappointment it had brought your father since it had happened, knowing that, while the family lawyers had kept the actual arrest quiet, the court case was always going to be public and a total media circus. How knowing that still hadn't prevented the *other shoe* thudding down onto your heart like a steel-capped boot when the conviction had finally gone public a fortnight earlier.

And, with it, your boyfriend's betrayal.

Though really she'd lived with that since the day it had dawned on her what Mark had done. And why.

He'd officially ended their four-month 'thing' while sitting in the arraignment waiting area at courtroom number four. As redundant exercises went it was pretty spectacular. What—other than his enormous male ego—made him imagine for a moment that she would want to be anywhere near the man who had set her up for arrest? The man who had betrayed her trust and used her for the publicity her name would bring to his animal-rights cause.

Though, truthfully speaking, she'd set *herself* up. She with her hopelessly optimistic expectations and lousy judgement. He'd just sealed the deal by holding the metaphorical door open for her to walk into the arms of the authorities.

'Crying is good for you,' she joked. 'Better out than in, right?'

'So that was...catharsis?'

'It was decompression. I've had a rough couple of months.' She struggled to keep it light. 'To be honest, you're lucky it didn't start at the airport. It was touch and go for a while there.'

He didn't understand. The three little lines between his eyebrows said so.

She tilted her head and studied him. Men were such alien creatures. 'I guess crying is unprofessional, too, huh?'

'I've cried,' he said, before thinking about it. A dark flush streaked up his jaw but he didn't shy away from the topic. 'But it didn't feel good.'

He struck her as a man who wouldn't appreciate her pity. Or her curiosity. So she didn't ask.

'I'm not in any trouble,' she confirmed instead. 'But thank you for the concern.'

It seemed so genuine—even if it was reluctant— Sera had to concentrate on not letting it birth a warm glow deep inside. It was his *job* to care. It wasn't personal.

It never was.

Grey eyes bored into hers, but then he must have decided to trust her. 'Okay. But remember—'

'I will come to you the moment I'm in any real need,' she pledged. 'Rule four. I haven't forgotten.'

He meant *risk* kind of need, of course. If she felt in any kind of danger. But it felt lovely—just for a moment—to think that she had someone to go to if her heart hurt or her head wanted to explode or something just really messed with her mind. An emotional storm home.

Usually she went to herself with that stuff.

'So what do you want to photograph today?' Brad asked, bringing them back onto a safer footing and dragging his gaze from hers back out to the desert.

Probably a good idea. How had things turned

from get-to-know-you chat to peering-into-your-soul chat so very quickly?

Sera pushed up straighter. 'Everything. Maybe we could start by exploring the grounds, do a bit of reconnaissance?'

He smiled at her clumsy attempt to speak his language. 'The entire fenced reserve is Al Saqr's grounds. It's fifteen per cent of all of Umm Khoreem. That's a lot of exploring. Wouldn't you rather take it a bit easy?'

'Nope. I plan on keeping nice and busy.'

'Most people generally relax over Christmas,' he hinted.

'I'm not most people.' But she reminded herself again that although he was a man he wasn't her father and he wasn't Mark. He didn't deserve her tension. He was just doing his job. 'And we have a whole month. Plenty of time for downtime, too.'

Then he asked her another question about her photography. And another. Pretty soon lunch was well and truly over, everyone that had been there when they arrived had left and a couple of new faces had arrived.

More couples... Ugh. How was she supposed to ignore the fact that she was alone during the holidays if Al Saqr kept throwing happy, lovey-dovey people in her face?

'If you want to get your camera out,' Brad finally said, standing and stepping to pull her chair from behind her as she did, too, 'we'd better get moving.'

She happily followed him.

This place was far too beautiful and bright to waste on thoughts of lonely Christmases and self-absorbed men.

CHAPTER FOUR

BRAD TRAILED CLOSE behind her, failing miserably at being invisible as Sera pottered about getting a feel for the late-afternoon light and the quality of images her tests were creating. The architecture, the exotic plant life, the wildlife. Aqil had warned her that the various hoofed creatures of the desert had free range within security fencing and they certainly let their curiosity off the leash by coming up here into the world of man. Not too close—smart things—but certainly close enough to photograph.

It took her nearly an hour to move the first one hundred metres from the restaurant.

Brad didn't complain once, though she saw him shifting his weight from foot to foot occasionally and each time he did she would self-consciously move a little farther along before becoming captivated by something else and halting again.

She moved off the paved pathways and onto the sand, wandering up and over the nearest dune to give herself the illusion of privacy from the other guests that occasionally passed by. Then her footprints—and the cascading patterns they created on the sand—kept her lens busy for another quarter-hour.

'Leave yourself something for tomorrow,' Brad murmured, out from behind his sunglasses.

'These are only test shots.' She smiled. 'I'm just getting a feel for how the sand and light work together.'

He nodded in the head-toss equivalent of an eye roll.

'You're welcome to go back to your pool, if you like,' she said.

That earned her a grunt, which she ignored and she kept right on photographing. The sun sank lower and lower and the light grew more and more gorgeous. But on the wrong side, really, to make the most of the intricate shapes drawn by the wind in the golden sand.

Morning. That was when this setting was really going to come alive.

It was only when she felt the little thrills spidering through her system that she realised how long it had been since she'd let herself be really excited by her photography. That had pretty much stuttered to a halt when she'd found herself in a fingerprint-processing queue.

'Okay, let's head back,' she said. 'I could do with another swim.' Something told her she'd be spending a lot of time in that pool.

It took just minutes to get to the suite because, despite spending hours taking pictures, they'd ended up just fifty metres from her door. Brad let her open it but pressed politely past and cleared the room before allowing her to enter.

It was hard not to grin as all that hard muscle squeezed past, brushing against her.

'What happens if someone kidnaps me out here while you're inside clearing the room?' she called in to him casually as he checked each of the outside-facing glass doors. Taking pictures was one way to pass the month ahead—messing with Brad's mind was another.

A girl had to have a hobby. And just because she didn't want to *touch* didn't mean that she couldn't sneak the occasional *look*, right?

'Calculated risk,' he called back from inside. 'Most people prefer to conduct their crimes in private. Anyone could walk past here and see you being bundled onto a getaway camel.'

Her lips twisted despite herself. There was

something almost alluring about the idea of being whisked away from the world on camelback—or on the powerful Arab horses that got their name from this peninsular—across all this sand, by some swarthy hottie. If he was built like Brad, she might not even scream for all that long.

He returned, waving her into her suite, and Sera plastered an innocent expression on as she stepped past him into the cool. His eyes narrowed immediately.

And that's why God invented fantasies. Because something told her flirting openly was most definitely outside procedures.

'I'm going to have a bit of downtime until sunset, then dinner as soon as it's dark,' she said not very subtly. Maybe a bit of healthy time apart would get her hormones back under control. Besides, jet lag was starting to catch up with her despite the restorative massage.

'Why don't you get something delivered here?' he suggested, reading her mind. Or maybe her body language.

Ooh. That was a good idea. A delicious meal on the pool deck.

He crossed to the writing desk and returned with

the glamorous menu folder. 'I'll call it in while you change for your swim.'

She pushed it back at him. 'Surprise me.'

One of the things she'd been looking forward to most about this trip was making fewer decisions every day. And trying new things.

She closed herself into the luxurious bathroom to slip back into her blue swimsuit. It had dried in about nine minutes flat after she laid it out on her deckchair, courtesy of the moisture-desperate desert air, and so now it was crisp and almost just-laundered fresh. Then she pulled out her hair ties and let her hair fall down her back.

One of the greatest joys of having long hair was feeling it hanging down your back, heavy and wet. It was just so…reassuring. Like a kind of hug.

Not pathetic at all, a tiny voice sniggered.

Needs must. When you grew up without your mother and were abandoned for months on end by your father, you took your intimacies where you could find them.

'Sera…?'

Speaking of intimate… Brad's voice sounded so close and so clear you would never know there was a thick, ornate, timber door between them. 'You want dinner on the deck or in the suite?'

Well… Wasn't that a cosy kind of question? Suddenly this whole set-up started to scream *couple*. The natural way he just integrated himself into her day, anticipating her needs. The way she'd adapted around him already.

On less than twenty-four hours' acquaintance.

'Deck, please. At sunset.'

His deep voice murmured, repeating her request for Aqil, presumably, and a wild thought rushed into her head about what that voice would be like breathing hard against her ear.

And just like that she tripped neatly across the line in the sand. The one between harmless imagination and dangerous indulgence.

'Just for one,' she called more urgently, stumbling over the phrase like the clunky, over-compensatory thing it was. The resulting silence screamed.

She froze, wincing, and caught her lame facial expression in the bathroom mirror.

You're the client, she told herself silently, giving herself a stern look. *You ask for whatever you want.* He'd painted such an unflattering image of women who got too attached to their personal security—well, okay, he'd only sketched an outline and she'd gone to cougar town with the image—

she didn't want him thinking that lunch today was anything other than some convenient company.

She wasn't desperate for his. She'd eaten alone plenty of times. Plenty.

It was pretty much the norm.

Still, she couldn't help trying to undo any offence she'd caused, calling out, 'I've got a date with some golden sands and a whole lot of silence.'

Her breath stilled while she waited and she refused to look at herself in the mirror again. Bad enough being a social klutz without watching yourself do it.

'It's okay, Sera,' Brad murmured, low, from beyond the door.

And it was. His voice said it was. He knew all along why lunch hadn't been a good idea and she was just slow catching on.

Okay, so his protocol was right.

That was awkward.

Brad helped himself to an off-duty beer from his minibar and flopped down on one of the two comfortable lounges on his deck.

The hotel staff who'd brought him his dinner had also taken the opportunity to draw every thick curtain in the place, creating a warm, cosy little nest for the night. The moment they'd gone and he'd quaffed his meal, he'd flung them all open again, inviting the darkness in. This was the part of working at Al Saqr that he loved the best. The vast skies at night. The darkness that only came with complete absence of the ambient glow that metropolises generated.

At least until the moon got higher.

He flicked his pool lights on, casting random little shapes on the canopy above his head as the cool night breeze played across the water's surface. It gave him about six feet of visibility beyond his pool.

To his left, a door closed loudly in the heavy silence, and it drew his busy mind to his neighbour.

Sera was a paradox, as clients went. Usually, it took him about a day to get a general lock on the personality of whoever he was watching, but she shifted as much as those sands out beyond the darkness. Confident and all about eye contact one moment, weeping in private the next. Sharp and bright in the SUV but sleepy and downright desirable with her mussed-up hair straight out of her massage. A clumsy kind of brittle when she'd told him she'd be having dinner alone, then full of awkward distress and kindness in trying to make good afterwards.

It was almost as if her tough exterior was at war with her softer, true self.

He dug around inside trying to identify the uncomfortable sensation and surprised himself by finding it. Wounded pride. Why? He never ate with clients; it was a chore he was thankful the rules prohibited. He watched clients while they ate, all the time. He inhaled a quick snack while they were in meetings or even the bathroom. But whole meals... He did those as he did most things—later and solo.

So why the bruised sensibilities just because a woman opted out of a second round of his tremendous company? Had he really grown that soft?

Or was he a little bit too intrigued by the paradox?

He placed his empty bottle onto the deck with one hand and peeled off his T-shirt with the other, then waded into the small, heated pool in his board shorts and let the water wash away the thought. The further the winter sun sank beyond the horizon, the faster the desert cooled around them until a layer of mist rose from the water and evaporated in the darkness.

Underwater, even the desert creatures were silenced, and he held his breath as long as he could to let the warm, watery cocoon leach the tension out of him. With the survival training he'd received in the Specials, that meant a long time.

He'd sought out the Sheikh's personal guard with an expectation that he'd get to be involved in some top-end protection tasks. Something that really exploited the skills he'd perfected in the military. Short bursts, complete strangers. Business types who were happy to treat him like a ghost. Or a shadow. Who relied on him for their safety but not for anything else.

Clients and short rosters that meant no chance of forging bonds.

That strategy had served him well these past two years. It had almost undone the damage of that day in Cairo. The day he'd learned the hard way not to get involved with clients.

Indifferent acquiescence...

Maybe he should get that tattooed somewhere prominent.

But four straight weeks of close contact with any client made things a whole heap tougher. And someone like Sera... Someone who pushed all his buttons. The one labelled 'intrigue'. The one labelled 'empathy'. The one labelled with a big red question mark...

Yeah, he needed to stay right away from that button, particularly.

Survival instinct forced him up above the surface eventually and he rolled onto his back and floated there, breathing deeply, losing himself in the changing shapes on the canopy above before finally hauling his dripping self out, towelling off and taking his empty bottle inside in search of a refill.

Sera witnessed the start of the oryxes' nightly migration as the sun started to sink below the dunes behind her suite. A little group of them had been lazing in the near distance all day in shallow, hoof-scratched divots in the sand around a waterhole but as soon as the shade vanished, so did they. They hauled themselves up, dusted off and began the long trudge...somewhere.

Over the hill and far away as the nursery rhyme went.

It made sense that oryxes and gazelles did all their resting during the heat of the day and their busy work in the cool of the night, and that changed things if she wanted to photograph them.

But it also made night-time a good time to head out onto the sand to explore without having to worry about the enormous, sharp-horned beasts lurking around the resort waiting to skewer themselves a Sera kebab.

She amused herself just metres from her darkened suite, photographing the extraordinary field of stars stretching out overhead—as if someone had spilled a tub of silvery glitter over the blackness above. More stars than she'd ever been able to see anywhere. It wasn't easy finding somewhere steady enough to stand her gear, and she'd dashed back inside to return with a field guidebook, a folded magazine and the empty plate that her stuffed date snacks had come on to wedge into the sand under her tripod's three feet. Then she'd settled down on the dune a metre or so away from her equipment as it took long, open exposure shots. They would be fun to play with on her laptop when it got too warm to be out on the sand.

A busy mind was a sane mind.

The longer she sat there, and the higher the moon climbed, the more her diminished human eyes could see. All around her, she was sure, were creatures that could see her as clearly as if she stood in daylight, while, to her, they were barely even shadows. Eventually she braved a bit more distance, getting a range of pretty night shots, including back at her own suite. She immediately regretted turning all her lights out because the gentle glow pouring out of suite eleven made for really pretty composition, but traipsing back up the dune to illuminate hers seemed like unnecessary hassle when Brad's fully lit and completely identical suite was empty. She could get some practice shots now and shoot hers tomorrow night.

She released her DSLR from the tripod, left her gear in a tidy pile in front of her pool and waded through the thick sand twenty metres to the left to frame up a shot of Brad's suite. A quick double-check through the zoom lens confirmed he wasn't resident, though he'd left a beer bottle out on his deck. He'd probably had a drink before heading up to the restaurant for his evening meal.

Meal for one, as she'd so clumsily stipulated.

Ugh.

With social skills like hers it was a miracle she'd ever managed to make friends at all. Let alone keep them. Though, some friends were more willing to indulge her social clunkiness, as it turned out. When it suited them. When there was some-

thing in it for them. That was as true in adulthood
as it had been in childhood.

Clever framing meant you couldn't see the bottle
in her shot, only the stunning little pool and the
softly lit suite beyond it. Green décor inside, where
hers was themed blue. She framed up the shot and
clicked, then tweaked a few settings in her camera
and readied to click again, trying to maximise the
saturation. But as her finger depressed the shut-
ter, the pool's still water shifted, then bubbled,
and then erupted with wet, male flesh as Brad
surfaced.

Not vacant at all!

She caught the yip of surprise before it grew
audible and dropped the camera down away from
her eye. But that didn't stop her seeing a more
distant Brad roll over onto his back in the water
of his pool and just…float. All peace and seren-
ity. Nothing like she'd seen him up until now. She
half spun away on polite instinct but her eyes were
slower to leave than her torso as Brad hauled that
big, tanned body out of the pool—water streaming down his back—and engulfed it in one of the
resort's massive towels.

Finally, her shoulders forced some decent manners on her and she sank onto the sand, her back

turned, and stifled a giggle as the adrenaline dumped from her system.

Trespass charges not enough, Sera? Looking to add 'stalker' to your criminal résumé?

Sheesh.

He hadn't seen her lurking out here in the dark. How could he? Not that *not* getting caught made her peeping any less Tom-ish…

Behind her, she eventually heard the clunk of Brad's suite door closing. Even at this distance, the silence amplified the simple snick as he went inside. She glanced back, sheepishly, when she heard the door again and caught him lowering himself back down onto the deck lounge, now dried and in loose jogging bottoms and a sweater, a fresh beer in one hand and a book in the other.

Oh… He was a reader.

Why did that throw her so much? Clearly, the man had to have an education to have come as far as he had in life. But being *able* to read didn't necessarily mean someone *liked* to read.

Brad did. And she hadn't expected that.

Though she wasn't sure what she had expected— she just wasn't used to getting to know much about the people who worked with her.

For her.

In the darkness, she twisted to her feet and returned to her camera equipment, where it still lay in front of her own suite. It didn't take long to become newly fascinated by the way the increasing moonlight slashed across the sand, highlighting the wind ripples that scarred all that eroded smoothness in a way that was totally different from the daytime. But while her fingers worked automatically, her mind struggled to engage. It was far too busy thinking about the momentary glimpse of Brad and his wet skin as he'd emerged from his pool.

On duty, Brad moved like a man on a mission. Every step considered, always scanning their surrounds, always as if he had somewhere important to be and was already late. Perpetually irritated. But off duty Brad just kind of…sauntered. He'd risen from the pool and then came back through those doors like a man who had nowhere better to be but on a deck drinking a beer and flicking through a crime novel.

She kind of liked it.

And she kind of wished she was on the deck lounge next to him doing the exact same thing. Just sitting in silence reading together. Chilling.

Then again hadn't she been wishing for much the same thing her whole life?

Don't get attached, her father would have cautioned; and wasn't that the pot calling the kettle a very gothic kind of black?

As if she needed to be told. As if she hadn't already learned not to attach to anyone, just in case. In her world, people came and went and always did their best but never, ever stayed. It was the nature of the beast. People who were paid for their services generally and eventually left for something else. They were staff, not friends—

'Sera!'

Mid-thought, hard hands spun her around and she faced a furious, puffing Brad.

'I'm less than a minute from the suite,' she automatically defended.

'In the dark. Alone!'

'I could see you,' she said, then flushed horribly at the admission. 'No way you wouldn't have heard me if anything had happened.'

'*Anything* could have happened in just the time it took me to get here,' he growled.

'Come on, not the getaway camel again.' Did he seriously think bad guys would turn up and drag her off into the desert?

'Vipers. Scorpions. One minute for me to get down here and two to carry you back up. That's three of the six minutes you get to live if bitten. This may be a resort but it's still wild habitat, skittering with things that can kill you.'

'Oh.' *Right.* She glanced down at her shadowed feet in the darkness.

'Why are you so resistant to simple instructions?' he gritted, fuming.

'They might be simple to issue but they're a lot harder to live by. I just wanted to get some night pictures.'

'Then you call me.'

'You're not my lackey, Brad. You've earned your downtime.'

'Then you get your night pictures tomorrow night and I take a few hours off in the middle of the day in lieu.'

Sure, it made sense when said like that. 'It doesn't work that way, Brad. When inspiration strikes…'

'Something tells me inspiration is always striking with you, Sera. My job is to keep you safe. Not to let you go traipsing off into death-infested sand dunes.'

'A little exaggerated, don't you think? I'm within a hundred metres of the suite. Give me a little credit.'

'I really want to, Sera, but we're not doing so well so far.'

There it was… The disappointment. Her father's judgement coming out of Brad's mouth. It never mattered what her intentions were…

'It's ninety seconds from safety,' she repeated, angrily, gathering up her gear and heading off back up the dune towards her suite.

Though, the ninety seconds it had taken to go downhill *did* take a lot longer in the cascading, scrabbling sands of uphill. By the time she reached the top and the little stony path into her suite's garden, she was puffing with more than just umbrage.

'I'm staying here,' Brad announced as she stepped up on deck and struggled to open her door with arms full of equipment. He pushed in and opened it for her.

'No, you're not,' she said as she squeezed past him. 'You have a perfectly good suite right next door.'

'Which I'll use when I'm confident that you're not going to make bad decisions.'

'You might as well pack your bags now, then, because I make bad decisions all the time. Apparently I'm on the perpetual verge of disaster at any given moment.'

If her father was to be believed, anyway.

He followed her into the suite until she spun back on him. Both her hands shot up between them and he walked straight into them. With only a thin sweater on, his chest felt every bit as hard as it had looked through her lens. She jerked her fingers away.

'You weren't serious?'

Grey eyes pinned her. 'Utterly.'

'You can't stay here.'

'Why not?'

Inspiration struck. 'Because it's against the law!'

It was the truth. And good luck convincing Arab authorities that a healthy, single man of his age took the sofa when spending the night in the suite of a healthy single woman of her age. Her eyes drifted to the massive bed just begging for two.

But her words definitely gave him pause. 'On your deck, then.'

'All night?'

'If it means I'm here the next time your muse calls, sure.'

The barely muffled hiss of air between her lips should have told him exactly what she thought of that idea. 'What's going to stop me simply going out the front door?'

He crossed to her dresser, took the oversized key from there and locked the front door from the inside, then pocketed the key.

Are you kidding me? First she was a prisoner within the resort and now within her suite.

'What if there's a fire?' She glared at him.

'I'll save you,' he shot back.

'How heroic.'

'I live to serve.'

Her camera bounced on the expensive mattress as she tossed it there. Behind her, he turned and moved towards the door.

'How am I going to sleep with you lurking out there?' she said, suddenly tired.

'Safely,' he barked.

He closed the glass door behind him, signalled at her to lock it from the inside, and then flopped himself down on the same deck lounge he'd been in one suite over when she'd gone all stalker on him. Automatically it became *his* lounge in her mind. She stood, glaring out at the back of his head, then gave up when it became obvious that he couldn't feel her irritation any more than he could see or hear it.

Fine. If he wanted to really play GI Joe, then he could. It was Arabia at the start of winter; he'd be cold overnight but he wouldn't freeze to death. Even for an Australian.

She snagged her pyjamas up as she passed the bed, took herself into the bathroom and changed, brushing her teeth and hair. As she came out, her glance went to the grumpy silhouette out on her deck rubbing his chilly hands against his jogging bottoms. He turned as she emerged onto the deck, a cushion in one hand and a woven throw from her sofa in the other. Without a single further word, she dumped both into his lap and then withdrew back inside, locked the door, yanked the curtains across and tried to block him from her mind as effectively as the curtains blocked the moonlight from the room.

CHAPTER FIVE

THE WHOLE NIGHTS on the deck thing became Brad's habit over the following week. Al Saqr was high-end enough that even the outdoor furniture was comfortable enough to fall asleep on. He'd lain on far poorer in his time. At least from the deck he could catch Sera the next time passion struck hard enough to draw her out of her suite on the quiet.

Not that it had happened again. Clearly, his presence was some kind of passion-killer.

Meh. He'd been called worse.

Over the days that had passed since he'd looked up from his book and seen a slight silhouette standing alone out in the moonlit desert, his nightly arrangement had grown from spare cushion and sofa throw to one of Al Saqr's fat European pillows, woven wool blanket, single beer, book and reading light. So, clearly, Sera had accepted that he was staying put. And her heart was too soft to let him just rough it.

No matter what she wanted him to believe by daylight.

Between her constant activity and cool aloofness by day and the staunch arm's length he'd been working so hard to maintain, it was amazing they managed to even meet each other's eye. Yet, by night, out came all the silent, borrowed comforts of home and Sera gave her true nature away.

Not brittle and sarcastic and angry all the time. There was compassion and empathy in there, too.

He shifted in his half-doze in the cold morning air and flipped onto his left side. A bare moment later, something drew his eyes open. The tiniest sound. A guttural kind of chuff. He squinted blearily in the golden glow that heralded sunrise.

Squinted and then blinked in astonishment.

A unicorn drank from the infinity edge of Sera's pool, white and luminous in the rich morning light, hazily obscured by the steam coming off the heated pool, shadows cast along its angular face, its long horn spiralling upwards to a deadly point.

Beautiful and completely impossible.

Brad cranked his head up away from the pillow, and the unicorn's shadowed eyes flicked in his direction. He froze. It kept right on drinking, though it didn't take its focus off the unexpected human. They went on like that—him freezing, it drinking—for minutes, and in those minutes the sun peered its wintry face over the horizon and the dawn light completely changed.

Those weren't shadows down its long, horse-like face—they were black facial markings. As if the light desert dew had spiralled down its black horn and stained its pristine face. And as it shifted more front-on he saw it was not one horn at all, but two. Just as long, just as sharp.

If the oryx was surprised to find a man sleeping on a pool deck at its favourite watering hole, it didn't show it, but when its eyes flicked away from his and locked firmly behind him, Brad couldn't help but follow their gaze back over his shoulder.

Sera stood there, half asleep and fresh from bed, her long fingers pressed up hard against the breath-frosted glass of her suite door, a look of childlike wonder on her face.

He should have been noticing her long, bare legs, or the shape of her breasts under her cotton pyjamas pressed hard up against the glass, or her just-woken bed hair. But—just like the oryx—he couldn't take his eyes off hers. The pure joy that glowed in them. She didn't run for her camera or even the sketch pad that sat on an easel near the door. She just…smiled. And stared. Radiant and transfixed. Completely oblivious to Brad's presence. Woman watched beast. Beast watched woman. And man watched woman. Even though he knew he shouldn't.

He really, really shouldn't.

Yet he didn't look away even as he acknowledged that thought.

Eventually the oryx wearied of her fascination and slurped its last mouthful. Brad only knew that from the shifting focus of Sera's mesmerised gaze as she followed the animal along the front of her garden and craned her neck to watch it disappearing over the edge of the dune, all watered up for the day. Only then did she turn her eyes to him, complete joy radiating from her face. The smile she threw him actually hurt his heart. She looked young. She looked alive.

She looked as beautiful and mystical as the unicorn.

And for that half-moment before she remembered she should, she didn't care that a virtual stranger was looking at her in her pyjamas. She just wanted someone to share the magical moment with.

Then, the real world intruded, the joy faded

slightly and she seemed to shrink away from the glass, reluctantly—almost against her own will—until all that was left of her was the opened curtains where she'd stood and the rapidly evaporating hand marks on the glass.

And all Brad was left with was the vague feeling that mornings would never quite be complete again without at least one unicorn…and without that gorgeously dishevelled face.

Sera was emerging from the bathroom when Brad's shadow fell across the deck doorway. He tapped on the glass first and then his watch. The doors, when she pulled them both inwards, invited the fresh, dawn air inside. It smelled as golden as it looked.

'You're still up,' he said.

Thank you, Captain Obvious.

'The falcons are on at seven a.m.,' she murmured. 'That's why I got up early in the first place.'

Up in time to see the oryx drinking at her pool.

'Glad you did?'

Okay, so he'd seen her in her brief PJs, unmade up, ungroomed and with sleep-encrusted eyes. Nothing she could do about it now. 'If you'd told me that was happening every morning I would have made more of an effort to be up for it before now.'

And be dressed.

'First time for me, too,' he admitted, stepping inside. 'Kind of cool, huh?'

That unexpected wildlife moment was to 'kind of cool' what these deserts were to just 'okay'.

'It didn't look that surprised to see me there,' he said. 'My guess is that he's been coming up in the dark each morning and stealth drinking while I've slept through it.'

'Why? When there's your empty suite right next door? And the one on the other side.'

'Creature of habit, maybe? Different humans might come and go in it but this is *his* pool...'

He certainly sauntered away from it with entitlement enough. In fact, he moved with the same kind of deliberate control that Brad did.

'Your buggy pickup will be here in ten minutes,' he said. 'I'm just going to run next door and change. I'll meet you at the front.'

He passed her the door key that he'd continued to hold on to and then jogged out the back, down past her pool and around the brush fencing between their suites.

If he took the full ten minutes, she didn't know it. She emerged from her suite as Eric pulled up in the courtesy buggy, and Brad was already standing at attention by the front door, casually but professionally dressed today in cargos and a light shirt.

'Morning!' Eric said to her cheerfully and with much more professional focus than the silent nod he'd just exchanged with Brad. 'How did you sleep?'

'Like the dead,' Sera admitted. 'Either it's the beds, the darkness, or you're drugging the water. I've never slept as well as I have here.'

Eric laughed. 'We try to keep guest-drugging to the minimum.'

'So, any chance that you'll be easing back on this crazy pace any time soon?' Brad murmured to Sera as they whizzed through the silent dawn towards the resort's heart. It was a reasonable question. She'd done half the resort's activities already— some of them twice—and filled every other waking moment with photography-related tasks.

'I've relaxed. Taken naps. Swims.'

He frowned. 'Taking photographs from the pool is not swimming.'

'But it is fun. And fun is leisure, right?'

From his grunt he was in no way convinced. 'I'm asking myself when you're going to stop pushing so hard. I'm also asking myself why?'

Why wasn't a conversation she felt like having before coffee. Or with a man who liked to be in charge so much.

She twisted to meet his gaze more directly. 'I'll stop pushing hard when this place and this desert stop being so interesting.'

'Right,' he muttered. 'So no time soon, then.'

They arrived at the centre of the resort and then Eric led them on foot to a mini amphitheatre set up on the sand. There, several birds of prey and a group of other guests waited for the daily flying demonstration. Customs confiscations of the bird variety, Eric explained as his colleague prepared the birds to fly. When someone tried to smuggle a trafficked bird in or out of the country and was caught, the bird was retired to Al Saqr. There, the valuable birds got to stretch their wings twice a day in training and lived like rock stars in between.

'They even have their own security,' Eric said for probably the hundredth time.

The smattering of other guests there all chuckled, but Sera couldn't help feeling self-conscious since her own security loomed like a bird of prey himself, two rows back from her on the richly carved wooden seating. She hoped Brad wasn't looking at the other guests with the same beady-eyed assessment that the bird did when its hood came off.

'This is a saker falcon,' Eric announced. 'The species after which Al Saqr takes its name. These birds have been flying desert skies for three millennia.'

They were, as she had expected, stunning, strong birds. Bullet fast. Each one went through its paces and showed off its strengths free-flying in a far arc around the amphitheatre and returning to try and snaffle their handler's fleshy lure. She learned about bird biology and habits, the valuable breeding efforts, the long history of falconry in the desert, and their personal history while each bird flew high up into the endless, blue sky, wheeling and turning, staying focused on its job. None of them tried to fly off although the tracking device clipped to their tether suggested they could have at any time.

Best of all, between each bird coming off its perch, Sera and the other guests got to take as many photos as they liked. *Boy, did she like.* Fortunately, her lens was long, her camera was digital and her memory card emptied so there was almost no limit to the number of up-close photographs she could take in the air or on the perch.

And then she met Omar.

'Omar is an eagle owl,' Eric narrated for the crowd, raising a healthy, solid, brown bird tethered to his gloved arm. 'He came to us as a chick and was hand-raised right here at Al Saqr. He never knew his parents. In fact, he's never really met another owl.'

Instant affinity formed in her heart for Omar.

She'd grown up in the care of others, too. She saw one parent several times a year—which was more than Omar could say—but even her father had only known her groupie mother for the time it took to get her pregnant midway through a European tour. Forty-two weeks later his lawyers had taken delivery of a squalling, infant Sera. He'd done his actual best and thrown all the money and personnel needed to raise a child at her, but touring half the year and recording offshore for much of the rest tended to put a crimp in any serious father-daughter bonding time. To give him credit, he'd worked hard to make the most of the time they'd had together but, when it was over, he went back to his busy, exciting life that passed in a flash, while she went back to her quiet, empty room to wait out the endless weeks until she got to wrap her spindly little arms around her daddy again.

'Omar looks like an owl, but he behaves more like a buzzard because that's who he grew up sharing an aviary with.'

Eric might have been talking about her. Except instead of growing up half buzzard, she'd grown up half...well, half grown-up. Even as a little kid, she'd been more like a miniature grown-up because that was who had raised her. A string of professional, well-trained adults out on her father's expansive country property. Big enough for a little girl to never tire of exploring and remote enough to satisfy her father's security concerns. Such was Blaise's fame at the peak of his career that even his young daughter was considered a credible target.

'He can't hoot,' Eric continued softly, curling a finger along Omar's glistening feathers, and earning sad sighs from his audience, 'because no one ever taught him how.'

Something in her fractured just a little bit.

Poor, hootless Omar.

When she'd finally hit thirteen and her father's obsessive popularity—and security concerns—had waned a little, she'd got to set foot for the first time inside an *actual* school filled with *actual* other kids. A reclusive, home-schooled rock heir fitted about as well there as Omar did amongst other owls. She'd had no real idea how to be a regular teen. The end result was a girl heavy on academic achievement but light on healthy friendships.

'He's had the best care here,' Eric assured everyone, on a charming smile, 'but we've all had to be super careful to make sure he didn't imprint on us. Because we could move on at any time and then where would he be if he'd cast one of us in the primary carer role? So he imprinted instead on the buzzard.'

The thing inside her that had fractured on discovering Omar's inability to sing the song of his people threatened to break even more. Break and spill out everywhere. Instantly, her body tightened up in anticipation and her pulse began to hammer. She shot to her feet, and Omar—with his super hearing and massive peripheral vision—flinched and ruffled his feathers in surprise. Eric threw her a concerned look.

Brad was there in a heartbeat, murmuring her name from just behind her ratchet-straight back.

'Headache,' she said for the benefit of the other guests who were starting to look at her. She mouthed an apology to Eric, who smiled and nodded and went back to his presentation. Then she climbed down off her seat and quickly scuttled away from the amphitheatre.

'Sera?'

Brad was right behind her. Of course he was. Perfectly positioned to witness her humiliation.

'Headache,' she repeated. Because lying was easier. How could she explain that a captive bird had opened up a sore spot in her chest. Clawed it open, really, with those big, taloned, completely innocent feet.

The sand dunes were steep just there, where the resort's main building towered over everything around them, and she sank as much as she climbed but, eventually, she neared the top. Her puffed breath wasn't made any easier by the fist twisting hard within her chest.

'Sera?' Brad jogged up closer. 'Are you upset about the show? The birds?'

'Why would I be?' she tossed back over her shoulder.

'I thought because of your thing for animals...'

She turned on the spot. 'My "thing"?'

'Your interest, in animal welfare...'

She could hardly blame Brad for the assumption.

She'd happily made her own bed when she'd innocently started photographing strays and waifs. And she'd more than lain in it when she was gullible enough to let Mark's PR-loving animal-rights group draw her into trouble by photographing the lab animals.

The tabloid headlines flashed before her eyes. *'Brazen Blaise...'* *'Rock Heir Faces Charges...'* And her favourite: *'Chip off the old Rock...?'*

That last one was the most ironic. Her father had spent his career bringing all manner of social injustice to light through his music; you'd think he would have been more supportive when she tried to do the same.

What did a girl have to do...?

'One bird didn't want to return to the wild and the other two couldn't make it. No, it doesn't bother me that they're living here, instead.'

'Then what's—?'

'Headache!' she shot back at him.

He clambered up the dune behind her. There was probably an easier path out of here but, right now, she just needed to be away from all the prying eyes—stat.

'Why don't we get you something to eat and drink?' Brad suggested, clearly at a loss for any better way of dealing with a neurotic female than feeding her.

The dark, quiet restaurant…with bathrooms. The female half of which was one of very few places in this whole resort where Brad could not follow her.

'Okay, yes.'

Near the dune's top he climbed past her, reached back and took her hand, hauling her up over its edge when her legs started to protest the steepest part. At the steps to the restaurant's deck she excused herself and didn't wait for his consent, plucking her fingers free of his.

'I'll just…freshen up.'

The facilities were as elegant as the rest of the resort and furnished just as authentically. The plush room smelled like a spice souk, which was a pleasant surprise given its usual purpose, but the delightful scent did nothing to ease the thoughts whipping around in her mind. As every other person in the resort was either still asleep or out on one of several early-morning activities, she had the whole place to herself, so she sagged down onto a padded chair recessed neatly off to one side and let her face fall into her hands.

We've all had to be careful to make sure Omar didn't imprint on us.

Was that how it worked? Enough love and affection for the bird's basic needs but not so much that a young Omar might have started growing attached.

We could move on at any time and then where would he be?

Right, because it was a job to them. And jobs changed. Thanks to her father's endless bank account and a revolving door of expert personnel, she'd made it to adulthood in one piece. Very nice people—professional and dedicated—but, ultimately, not hers to keep. In the same way that the staff at Al Saqr cared for Omar but took pains that he didn't come to *need* them. To rely on them. To *love* them.

In case they had to leave.

Having her life summed up in such matter-of-fact terms this morning... Looking at Omar's sweet face and hunched over body—*poor hootless Omar*—it had just felt too raw.

A quiet knock sounded on the door.

'Coming!'

Sera shot to her feet and crossed to the row of sinks and flicked on one tap. It took only a moment to wash her hands and rinse her face. A moment longer to dry them on a scented, fluffy towel that felt too good to throw straight into the waiting hamper. She took a few more moments, steeling herself before emerging to Brad's intent stare. He shepherded her into the restaurant and pulled out a chair for her at a table on the deck. Seeing the golden sands and bright morning light made her feel a little better, but seeing the people streaming away from the finished bird presentation at the foot of the dune below made her feel a little worse.

She'd missed out on photographing Omar.

Brad pulled out the chair opposite her.

She took a long breath. 'I'd like to—'

'Eat alone,' he finished for her. 'I know. I'll move as soon as I'm sure you're okay. Do you need a doctor?'

In fact, she'd been about to say, *'I'd like to apologise…'* For her rapid departure from the falconry display. And her general neurosis. And her crankiness all week.

'For a headache?' The lie was catching up with her and shame was close on its heels. 'It's just the sun.'

'It's only just gone seven.'

'Then I guess I'm tired.'

'You told Eric you slept like the dead.'

'Brad—'

'Sera?' His grey eyes bored into her. 'Come on. I'm not leaving you until I know for certain that you don't need me.'

She stared at him, trying to decide how much to share. Hadn't he said she should come to him? This might not have been what he'd meant but right now it was exactly what she needed.

Someone to confide in.

'Omar,' Sera started, lines of tension forking at the corners of her eyes.

It took Brad a moment to realise who she meant. 'The owl?'

'I just… His story got under my skin.'

An *owl* had caused the dramatic public exit? Though staying and bursting into tears would have been more dramatic and that still looked like what she wanted to do. Did her emotions always run so close to the surface?

'His situation resonated for me,' she continued.

Brad frowned back at her. 'What about it, particularly?'

'No one taught him how to hoot.'

He took the menus from the young man who presented them but placed them straight down to focus on what she was saying. The waiter took the hint and dissolved into the background.

'He seems to have survived well enough without it,' Brad said, scrabbling desperately to connect the dots.

'He's an owl, Brad. He's supposed to hoot.'

Somewhere in here was a point she was trying to make if he could just find his way to it. 'Sera, he doesn't know any other owls, so he doesn't know that owls *should* hoot. I doubt he feels any kind of deficiency.'

Her brown eyes bled indecision back at him. But then they seemed to clear, and she took a deep breath.

'Has anyone stopped to think that they've raised a bird bereft of a personal attachment to anyone at all? Not just to them.'

His chest tightened. 'Okay...?'

'The way I was brought up—by nannies and tutors and bodyguards... Do you think any of them stopped to think that if they weren't teaching me how to hoot then no one was?'

Oh. This was about her childhood.

'Maybe they were looking out for your best interests?' he said tightly, because he *was* one of those people she was talking about. And he knew all about the firm line in the sand that they weren't supposed to cross. He'd juggled it his whole working life. So a crack at them was a crack at him.

'How exactly is it in a child's *best interests* to be kept at arm's length?' she argued.

How? He could tell her some stories. One in particular…

'If they got too attached—'

'Oh, don't get me wrong,' she hurried on, 'I eventually came to appreciate the professional distance. When I was old enough to understand it. It meant my heart didn't get broken every time I said goodbye to a paid staffer.' She took a deep breath. 'But try telling seven-year-old me that.'

He fought to keep his jaw from locking up, it was that tight. He could understand what it must have been like for her when she was a kid. But she had no idea what could have happened if any of her team had let themselves get too close. And why they didn't.

Or weren't supposed to.

'What if I'm like Omar?' she tried again. 'Deficient without realising it. What if there are things normal women do that I don't know I should be doing?'

Like hooting. It was then that he finally realised what she was getting at.

'Normal women?'

She waved a single hand. 'Women raised in normal families. By normal parents.'

'Instead of being raised by rock-star millionaires in rambling rural retreats?'

Her laugh scraped like steel wool. 'Instead of being raised in a bubble by paid professionals.'

She leaned in over their unopened menus. 'You must have dated loads of women...'

Okay...enough. He needed to put this to rest. 'Sera. Normal doesn't exist. People are different. That's what diversity is all about.'

'But on a scale of one to ten. How do I rank?'

He lifted one brow. 'Against the ocean of women I've apparently been with?'

But she didn't waver. She truly thought that her upbringing had turned her into something...broken.

He sat back, frustrated. 'You want a number?'

'Yes, please.'

He pursed his lips in exaggerated thought. 'I'd give you a...four.'

'A *four*?' Her shocked cry drew the waiter's eyes.

He stepped forward then froze again as the privacy of their discussion dawned on him. 'Out of ten?'

'Maybe a five on a good day.'

All she could do was blink at him. He leaned forward earnestly.

'Your talent as a photographer isn't normal,' he said. 'The way you can switch between personalities in the space of a breath isn't normal. The way you are put together is a mile from normal.' *God knows!* 'Your interest in the most invisible details of life isn't normal. Your ability to have a discussion like this and then go right back to polite strangers isn't normal.'

She frowned at him, probably trying to decide whether she was being insulted or not.

'I've known women who didn't get passionate about anything. Ever. Or they faked excitement in things that I liked to make themselves more appealing. They could look at this desert and see nothing more than sand and sun, and this trip as nothing more than a chance to get a tan. You want me to rate you against them?'

She blinked at him. 'Why are you so angry?'

Good question. But there was something incredibly disturbing in the idea that anything those people did raising Sera might have turned such a strong, accomplished woman into this uncertain, weepy mess.

Because he'd *been* one of those people. And he'd had his own little Sera.

'I've known women who are the most extraordinary mothers and who would give their lives for their children. Or battlers of terrible diseases. You want me to rate you and your privileged life against them?'

Her lips tightened. 'Privilege is not all it's—'

'How about the women soldiers who can shoot a man in the face without blinking?' he barged on. 'Where should I rank you against them?'

Her arms curled around her middle. 'Look, forget I—'

'There is no normal, Sera,' he said, softer, seeing the impact his frustration was having on her. 'There is no scale. The only way Omar the owl would know that his inability to hoot is a *deficiency* is because we tell him it is.'

'And it isn't?'

Brad shrugged. 'What's he going to do with a hoot? Use it to call for an owl girlfriend he'll never get to meet? Use it to defend territory that's already protected for him? Omar's life is what it is and, in his life, a hoot is an optional extra. He's getting along just fine without it.'

The pinch of her face got tighter and he thought for a moment that she was going to splinter.

'He's not broken, Sera, or disabled.' *You're* not. 'Being different is what makes him so memorable to all the people who meet him. Who do you think they go home and tell stories about to their families and whack on their social-media pages? The other birds? It makes him more special, not less.'

Something in his words pulled the plug on all the morning's tension and it just poured out, over the deck and down onto the dune below them like so much sand.

'He's not hootless.' She sighed, finally getting it. 'He's just… Omar.'

'Exactly.'

Which meant Sera wasn't necessarily deficient either. Despite her upbringing. She just…was. And he really needed that to be true because God help him if his actions had caused this kind of distress to the boy he'd been responsible for.

Sera's brows dropped. 'Have I annoyed you?'

He took a deep breath and marshalled his emotions. 'No.'

'Then what is that face?' she challenged.

He considered her, long and hard. Whether or not she was up to hearing any more of his potted wisdom.

'Everyone has baggage, Sera. Everyone. We are all products of our upbringings, but those things shouldn't steer our actions forever and they're not excuses for whatever mess we might have made of our lives.'

She sat back straighter, and a coldness whipped around between them even in the warmth of the desert morning. The chill of his judgement.

'Tell me about the trespass,' he demanded, out of nowhere, and he suddenly realised that he really wanted to know. Needed to know.

Her eyes narrowed slightly. 'Tell me about your interest...'

But he couldn't. Not when he didn't understand it himself.

He placed his hands flat on the table, readying himself to get up. 'You're right. It's none of my business. I'll leave you to your breakfast.'

'Don't.' The word shot out of her like a bullet. 'Sit. Stay.'

He glanced back down at her. 'So, I'm your dog now? Maybe I should get you a whistle?'

'Stay,' she repeated, more softly, and her chocolate eyes filled with remorse. Long fingers reached across to his side of the table and pressed there. 'Please.'

He did, though it took him long enough to decide.

The hovering waiter seemed relieved to finally secure their order and it wasn't long before Brad's protein-rich breakfast was delivered, steaming, along with her platter of local curiosities. In between mouthfuls they talked about the oryx from this morning, the beautiful birds they had just seen, and how she could go to the bird-of-prey training every day for the rest of the month if she wanted to photograph Omar properly. At first, it was a bruised kind of conversation—as though both of them were a bit raw and confused as to how things had gone so awry just moments before—but the longer they went, the easier it became.

Though, *easier* wasn't the same as *easy*. Something about Brad kept her always just one step shy of relaxed.

'I thought we were working towards rehoming ex-lab animals,' she suddenly volunteered as the waiter who refreshed their final coffees departed. 'Legitimately.'

He had no trouble keeping up with her sudden

tangent. And she thought he looked relieved that she hadn't entirely dismissed his interest. Even if she didn't understand it. 'You didn't know you were trespassing in an unauthorised space?'

'I should have. I accept that as my responsibility.' She shrugged. 'I mistook politics for passion.'

'Explain that.'

Technically, he had no real right to ask—it had no bearing on his ability to do his job—but the past half hour had earned him at least one indulgence. Even if it was to discover her least fine moment. But boiling months of sorrow down to twenty-five words or less wasn't easy.

'I trusted the wrong people. Friends. A lover. And it turned out they were more interested in my connections than my photographic abilities. The end.'

'A lover?' Trust him to grab onto that. 'Mark Ryder?'

Hearing his name still made her heart twinge, but not for good reasons. She squirmed against the necessity to reveal her own naïveté. 'How do you know about Mark?'

'Your file,' Brad said, simply. 'He was underlined. Twice.'

'That's more prominence than he deserved, as it turns out.'

'What happened?'

'He thought there might be some PR advantage in being with me. For his animal-rights cause.'

'He was right,' Brad murmured. 'That story went global. Effected real change for those animals.'

Air struggled to push past the fist in her chest. 'Yes, it did.'

Though at her cost.

'And now you're lying low in the desert while it blows over?'

He made that sound so cowardly.

'The timing was not good,' she muttered. 'The band was launching a new album for the Christmas market—'

'Wait…' His large hand came up and his grey eyes turned stormy. 'You've been exiled here, practically under guard, because your father doesn't want his downloads impacted by bad press?'

'"Upstaged",' she quoted. 'And it was more his music label's idea…'

But the defence sounded weak even to her ears. There had definitely been more than one point where she'd hoped her father would have backed her. Even against the label's powerful executive.

She'd only ever wanted his respect, but it was getting harder and harder to capture that. If she ever had.

'Dad asked me to do this. So...here I am. Trying not to disappoint him.' She took a deep breath. 'Though your presence unfortunately means that he doesn't trust me not to.'

If he had, he never would have had their London security arrange protection here in Umm Khoreem.

Brad flopped back against his seat. 'No wonder you haven't exactly warmed to me. I must be a daily reminder of that.'

Hourly.

'I'm sorry if I've been...un-warm,' she murmured. 'It's really none of your fault.'

He laughed. 'I was so sure I was a likeable guy. Is it wrong that I'm relieved?'

She smiled at him, then lost time as his laugh sobered into a warm gaze. But he dropped his head and made busy with folding his table napkin, which meant she could breathe again.

'End of day, his people wanted me out of London while the media attention blew over and I was happy to go. I'm not a big fan of Christmas anyway, but this year The Ravens have been booked to perform for some US millionaire.'

'So your father is spending the holidays with someone else's family?' Brad shook his head.

'And doing a New Year gig in New York while they're over there.'

'That sucks.'

The succinct truth drew a laugh out of her. 'Nice summary.'

Though, in reality her father only ever made it home one Christmas in three, anyway. But when he did, everything else was forgiven. Apparently she was still seven years old at heart.

'Is that why you picked an Arab region to lie low in? Because December twenty-fifth is just another day?'

She couldn't hold his eyes then. She turned hers back out to the golden sands. 'That was the plan.'

'Well, London's loss is Al Saqr's gain,' he commented. 'Though I should warn you they don't completely ignore it here thanks to the overseas visitors. There will be festive menus at the very least.'

Her laugh tinkled as much as the cutlery of diners around them. 'If it's not "Jingle Bells" on the radio and heart-warming movies on the TV, I'm happy enough.'

Brad considered her for an age, until she started to squirm under the scrutiny. 'What?'

'Just trying to imagine what happy looks like on you.'

Anyone could be forgiven for confusing the heated glow spreading out from her solar plexus under Brad's close regard for happiness. Or the look in his eye for something more than just empathy. But she wasn't that easily fooled.

She folded her napkin and laid it quietly onto the table.

'If you do see it, let me know. We can be amazed together.'

CHAPTER SIX

THE HEAD OF Security was going to kick his butt. His boss was starting to get twitchy at the latitude Brad was employing in watching over Sera—the cosy dining, the nights on the pool deck—not because he couldn't see that he was doing what was necessary for the job, but because he'd never known Brad as anything but the poster child for discipline. The guy who coloured strictly within the lines.

Then again, Brad was getting twitchy himself. He'd learned the hard way not to get friendly with his clients. But every day with Sera made it more and more difficult not to bend rules.

Try telling seven-year-old me that, she'd said and painted such a vivid picture of her lonely childhood, he'd struggled not to see another little face superimposed over his image of seven-year-old Sera. The last thing he needed was to be drawing comparisons between Egypt and Sera. Or to empathise for the situation with her father.

Empathy led to compassion.

And compassion wasn't going to get this job done.

He moved up behind her as she stepped over the threshold into the resort's heart to meet her guide. Standard procedure even though they'd been here long enough now to know where to go to meet Eric for just about anything. Today it was camel riding. She'd been waiting for a quieter guest day when she'd have the sands—and the camels—more to herself. He guessed that getting the kind of shots she wanted wasn't easy when there was a dozen pairs of feet trampling over everything. It took a full week and a half before a day fell where only one other couple happened to book a desert sunset ride.

That was about as good as it was going to get.

'Well, hello...!' Sera gushed.

You'd think she was greeting a pack of puppies. The cud-chewing camels knelt in a five-long, curved train, and a loose one stretched out in the sand just beyond them like a gangly, oversized dog. The four in the middle were fully kitted up in the camel equivalent of saddlery complete with patterned woven throws and bright, woven muzzles over their mouths. The front camel and the reclining one had no saddles at all, just a thick wad of rugs folded onto themselves and held on by a couple of girth straps. At first glance, the camels all seemed to be identical—pale, leggy ships of the desert. Up close, they were distinctly different: Sera's was honey coloured where the one behind was more wheat. His had a stately head where its neighbour's head was longer. All of them had the deep, silently considering eyes of their species. With supermodel lashes.

Eric took all four of them through a basic safety talk and then gave Sera his arm to help her mount. With her camel kneeled, she barely needed the assistance. She grabbed the saddle, pushed up onto her elbows and swung her forever legs over the pommel like a gymnast. Brad waited while she got herself comfortably secure, passed her camera pack up, then walked behind to his own animal and hiked himself on.

Salim, the camel driver, worked his way down the line checking everyone was secure. When he got to his side, Brad caught his eye and murmured, 'Extra care today.'

Salim lifted one brow, glanced at Sera and nodded.

'Relax, Brad,' Sera quipped, misreading his tension. 'If anyone tries to steal me away on their camel I'll just outrun them on mine.'

Behind them, Eric nudged his sleeping young animal onto its feet and leapt on as if he'd been born to it. Salim *was* born to it, and he did the same up front, sitting way back on his mount and half hooking his leg around its blanketed hump in a relaxed side-saddle that lent itself best to his traditional robes. Immediately behind Salim, the couple got all settled on their shared animal.

Poor Sera…*another* couple.

The thought came before he could shut it down. There was no 'poor' Sera. Or happy Sera. Or cranky Sera. For his own sanity there could only be client Sera. That was just how it had to be.

And how he wanted it.

Salim gave a whistle and all five animals in his train stood, back ends first.

The best part of riding a camel—their legs seemed to be jointed the wrong way and they pushed up with their knees while taking their weight on their elbows, then righted their front halves. Except they took their sweet time about it. Salim gave Sera's camel a shout when it lingered just a bit too long in elbow phase and she and her expensive camera gear wobbled precariously. Brad's eyes instantly went to the soft sand below and he started thinking about impact consequences until the surly beast stood up fully and she was able to release her white-knuckled grip on the pommel behind her.

Her feet sought around for something to brace in and eventually give up at the lack of stirrups and just dangled uselessly. He knew the feeling. Stirrups gave you balance and strength and the ability to leap off responsively if you had to. You were a *participant* in stirrups. You were just a passenger without them.

The only power no stirrups gave you was the power to tumble off into the sand face-first.

The couple squealed a bit and then they were off, Salim urging his lead animal to a comfortable lope and all others following lazily. Eric gave the train a moment to straighten up then jogged up from behind to ride next to Sera. Every muscle fibre in Brad's body tightened, even as his brain told him it was just Eric and he was paid to engage her. And even as his brain assured him that the only reason he was getting tight-chested about it was because *he* was paid to do so.

He was her protection. He was supposed to feel protective.

But not possessive, a tiny voice judged.

'It's so beautiful,' Sera called back to him once Eric had finally trotted off, gripping tightly with her knees as her camel swayed from side to side in its exaggerated gait, so that she had both hands free to wrestle her gear out of its bag. Along the train, their fat-filled humps lolled in syncopation but once they hit a rhythm he saw her relax and enjoy the journey out into the dunes as the sun sank ever lower on the horizon. Conversation wasn't really an option given they were all facing the front and spread along the train, but that didn't stop Sera turning and smiling back at him at regular intervals across the twenty minutes it took to get out to their break point.

He hardened his heart against every one.

On arrival at the base of a massive dune, Eric and Salim helped the couple up front until they stood beside their now kneeling mounts. Brad gave his camel a hearty pat on its thick hide and then strode forward to relieve Sera of some of her camera gear so she could climb down.

'You really need to get yourself a little point and click,' he murmured, wrangling the heavy gear.

She turned her outrage down to him. 'Wash your mouth out!'

But then her pleasure in the journey spilled over in a tinkling laugh as she sprang to the ground. 'Come on.'

As he trailed her past the front of the camel train his eye line collided with Salim's. Both of them tore their focus away to something else.

The dune ahead was hard and compacted at its core but as loose as the sand around the resort on its surface. That made scrabbling up the outside a heap trickier than a regular hill climb, so that when they arrived midway up where a catering station had been set up for sunset drinks they were both out of breath.

'Water or sparkling wine?' Eric asked Sera, easily slipping from guide mode to host mode and holding one of each up in his hands.

Sera reached for the frosty-glassed champagne.

Eric tossed the bottle of water to him.

'I think that's the first drink I've seen you have since you got here,' Brad murmured. He'd assumed she didn't drink, but maybe she was actually worried about the local prohibitions. None of which applied within Al Saqr's fences.

'We're standing in the middle of the Arabian desert,' she said on a long, relaxed breath. 'The sun is setting and stars are going to start twinkling. Can you think of a better time to enjoy a quiet glass of bubbles? Besides, weren't you the one who wanted me to chill out a bit?'

'Yes, I was.' He laughed. 'Maybe I should get you a second glass.'

He glanced at the couple who were already in full romance mode, making their way to the top of the dune, champagne in hand. Sera took a sip and then started to make her way to a sunset-facing point about three-quarters of the way up the dune.

Brad set off after her. 'Here...'

He relieved her of her glass in exchange for her camera gear he still carried, and she thanked him with a comfortable smile then got busy taking her first test shots. The sun still had a reasonable way to go before it hit the horizon but the light changed fast out here, meaning constant adjustment of the settings on her camera. So, she was right to hurry. Every now and again, he passed her the wine and she took a grateful, sighing sip before getting busy behind the camera again.

'Is that pollution?' she asked, looking up at the fine haze way up in the troposphere that cast an ethereal pink glow over everything as the sun drew closer to the distant horizon.

'It's sand,' he explained. 'It blows out to sea by

day but returns on the evening currents. The price of living in a desert nation.'

Her smile, then, rivalled the sunset that bathed her in its beautiful light, and he had to take a long, strong breath to settle his pulse as she turned back to her work. 'It does great things for my photos.'

A dozen glowing, golden dunes stood between their vantage point and the distant resort and each one of them began to change shape as the sun sank towards the horizon. The closest ones almost rippled with the wind-born striations across their surface. Easy to see why people called it a sea of sand. Beyond those, the tiny Bedouin-style suites of Al Saqr and—beyond those—the blazing, enormous sun as it kissed the western horizon. Sera's camera whirred away, capturing all of it. She photographed down low, she photographed from the highest dune point, she photographed the straggly fire bush that was home to the creatures that wouldn't come out until dark. She forgot all about her champagne as she grew more and more engaged.

Up on the top of the dune, the couple that rode with them on the camel train stood silhouetted, in some intimate conversation. Sera surreptitiously turned her camera and fired off a few shots against the gentle pink twilight before the two strangers wrapped each other in a long, enduring hug.

And then the sun was completely buried in the sands of the horizon. And everything changed.

What was previously pink washed over with a purpley-blue and the definition all around them diminished. The man staffing the drinks stand fired up a pair of bright brands that flickered and burned and, from nowhere, he produced a platter of delicious hors d'oeuvres.

Brad laid a hand on Sera's lens and lowered it.

'Enough,' he said mildly. 'You're missing all the good stuff.'

She didn't protest, glancing around behind them at the changed desert as if she'd just awakened from a nap. She packed her gear away in its bag, took back what little was left of her champagne and followed him back down to the food-station area where delicious aromas of goat's cheese and onion, sizzling meat on mini skewers and a trio of earthy dips and salted bread awaited.

'I'm going to email you a couple of images to the resort's address,' she said quietly to Eric, glancing at the silhouetted couple. 'Could you please make sure they get to them? They might like a memory of the proposal.'

Eric nodded and smiled and then drifted off again.

'That was a proposal?' Brad asked when he was gone. 'How could you tell?'

She turned and glanced at him strangely. 'How could you not?'

Okay, so…yeah. It had been a pretty schmaltzy scene and these views would be hard to top as proposal memories went. In fact, with Eric and the couple's guide tactfully withdrawn, the fire brands of the food station flickering like oversized candles, and Sera no longer otherwise engaged with photographs, the whole thing suddenly took on a whole bunch of extra meaning.

Extra awkward *romantic* meaning.

'So what's the plan for tomorrow?' he said a bit louder than necessary.

Sera just smiled at him as if she knew exactly how uncomfortable he'd just become, but she wasn't going to buy into his idiocy. She squeezed his forearm and moved past him to the catering table to nibble on some of the goodies there. He did his whole standing-to-attention thing not far behind. But with the guides keeping polite distance and the couple immersed solely in each other, Sera had no one to talk to if not him.

And suddenly he got a vivid flash of what her childhood might have been like. When the only people around were there because it was their job to be. When she had no one to share experiences like this with.

Don't be a jerk, Kruger. Talk to her.

'Want to go meet the camels?' he asked instead. It wasn't ideal but it was a reasonable compromise between too alone and too together.

Her eyes brightened in the glow from the brands and she nodded enthusiastically. A soggy kind of satisfaction swelled in his gut, and he realised that it pleased him to please her.

He took her gear again so she could finish eating the few nibbles she'd grabbed and walked beside her as she picked her way carefully down the dune face. Salim had lit the brands at the foot of the dune, too, and his animals were bathed in a rich red glow. As they approached, two camels grunted in protest.

'No, we're not getting back on yet,' Sera reassured them loudly, warmly. She crossed straight to Salim.

'Would it be okay to say hello?' she asked him.

Salim glanced at him for only a moment before rising from his rest on the warm sand and replying.

'They would be delighted.'

Meeting the camels formally was lovely but wouldn't have been nearly as notable if Brad hadn't dropped back and given her and the camel driver so much space. Normally he trailed her like a con-joined twin, but out here—where there had to be more risk, not less—he fell back into the night's shadows while the camel driver introduced her to his charges.

And his absence got her attention.

'Do they have names?' she asked.

Salim pointed at each animal in turn and rattled off their Arabic names as well as discussing their personalities and then answered a few more of Sera's questions about their care and management.

'Your accent is very good,' she commented when he finished.

'I was raised speaking it as well as the language of the Bedu,' he murmured with another anxious glance towards Brad.

Sorry, friend, looks like he's leaving us to it.

Salim bowed politely and backed away, looking

quite relieved and leaving her to commune with the camels. She wove in between each kneeled animal, patting their long faces and looking deep into their thickly lashed eyes, chatting lightly to them and making mental notes for images she might be able to get on a future desert trek. Her treads in the thick sand were silent and so, as she came quietly around the back of the camel nearest to Brad, she caught him and the camel driver, heads down, in private conversation.

They practically sprang apart when they saw her. It was the first time she'd seen Brad even slightly off guard. But before she could speak, voices began to filter down the dune towards them.

Moment lost.

But her curiosity blazed as bright as the torches poking up out of the sand.

It took about ten minutes to get the reluctant camels back on their feet and everyone mounted in the dwindling light. Brad seemed conscious of her speculative gaze falling on him—and, occasionally, on the camel driver—but, finally, she was mounted up between them and couldn't plague either of them with her curiosity.

The wide rocking motion of the camel helped to dislodge some of her inquisitiveness on the return journey, but it came back in force as soon as they got back to the resort. Sera warmly thanked the camel driver—who only met her eyes for the moment it took to be polite—then farewelled Eric. Brad stood silently at guard throughout. He did a cracking impersonation of the camel driver's averted gaze.

Okay, what was going on...?

She headed back up towards the suite, glancing at him repeatedly. But his face was closed and his forward-facing eyes kept her firmly out. Eventually she sped up to get a little ahead of him, spun and planted her feet in front, saying nothing, just staring with eyebrows raised.

'So...that was rude,' she began. Not really where she wanted to start the discussion but it was as good a lead-in as any.

Tension seemed to make him taller. 'What was?'

'Your failure to thank the camel driver. Or even acknowledge him.'

Brad's night-darkened eyes narrowed. As if he knew when he was being played. 'He'll survive.'

'Anyone would think you had an issue with the man.'

'Are you truly calling me on my cultural sensitivity, Sera? The woman who arrived in the country wearing a glorified table napkin and scandalised half the arrivals lounge?'

'Technically, I'm calling you on your shadowy secrecy, but clearly you aren't getting that.' And she knew Brad well enough by now to recognise deflection when she saw it. 'Come on, what gives?'

She'd meant this interaction to be playful teasing but the sudden defiance in Brad's expression turned it very quickly into something a whole lot less fun.

'What gives,' he repeated, 'isn't really any of your business, Sera. Like most of the questions you ask.'

She stumbled back half a step and then steadied. 'Right you are.'

She turned back towards the resort's hub, powered past it and headed to their suites. On arrival, she waited silently while Brad opened up and cleared the room, then brushed past him and laid her camera gear down.

'I'm going to skip dinner,' she announced, trying to keep her body language loose to beat his stupid specialist training. She'd grazed on the table out in the desert and she had a bowl full of fruit in here. She wasn't going to die overnight. And he wasn't her keeper.

'Okay,' he murmured. Making no effort at all to keep her.

'I'll see you tomorrow.'

His grey eyes turned steely. 'All right.'

But he just stood.

And she just stood.

One of them had to move first.

'I'll leave you a beer on the deck,' she tried again. As hints went, it was not very subtle.

That drew his eyes to the curtains the service staff had pulled closed. Something told her tonight would be the first night she left them that way. Speculation bubbled across his expression, followed by exasperation. But he knew his professional manners and—boy—was he ever master of his emotions.

'Okay, Sera. See you in the morning.'

The moment he left, shame flooded her body. Snoop's remorse. Brad was right, it really was no business of hers what stood between him and the camel guy. Her curiosity was piqued but she was hardly going to lose any sleep over it. There was just something so...*unjust*...about his expectation that she would bare all in their conversations and yet he would remain such a closed book. The harder he fought to keep his secrets, the more she came to resent them. On principle.

She didn't even want to know what they were. She just wanted him to trust her with them.

Is that it? a little voice challenged. *Or do you just want to know that* you *can trust* him?

You'd think that she would have sworn off that by now. She'd trusted Mark and his friends and it had turned out they were anything but worthy of her trust.

Worthy...

The word echoed around her brain. Was that what she was doing with Brad? Testing his worthiness? The aspects of him that he wasn't already paid to deliver? Pushing him to see how he stood up? Why, when he was around for only a few weeks at best?

She sagged.

She really had learned nothing since her childhood.

The woman was infuriating.

Brad sank down onto the deck chair and tossed back half of a beer he didn't really even want. But keeping his hands busy would stop him from going back in there and picking a fight. So if nothing else it served that purpose.

The more he tried to keep Sera at bay, the harder she seemed to work to wiggle her way under his defences—consciously and unconsciously. As if a woman who'd been neglected by her father and been thoroughly betrayed by her jerk of a boyfriend needed any help at all in garnering his empathy.

Now she had him feeling like a louse for maintaining the boundaries he was *required* to observe.

Visiting Salim's camel train had been a bad idea; putting the two of them in the same space for any amount of time was always going to lead to questions—on both sides—but desperate times called for desperate measures. In that moment, it was find a solid distraction or haul Sera into his arms for a hug. She'd just looked so lost and so lonely standing there on the dune side.

Not the first lost, lonely soul he'd carelessly let himself soften to.

How exactly is it in a child's best interests *to be kept at arm's length?* Sera's words on the day of the flight show returned to him just as hard now. Like a punch to the guts. He'd been burning to tell her that it wasn't necessarily in a child's best interests for them to be drawn close either.

It wasn't good for a kid named Matteo. It nearly got him killed.

Building a friendship with someone who was only going to be in your life for a nanosecond wasn't going to do Sera any good either. Not with the kind of childhood and revolving door of caretakers that she'd had. Her comment on the drive out here—*'just so I know you're real'*—made a whole lot more sense given the supposed friends who'd roped her into their animal-rights protest. Who'd used her celebrity to get themselves some publicity. And all the people she'd been raised by who all kept a professional distance.

But, clearly the whole *indifferent acquiescence* thing wasn't really working out. Sera was under-skilled in acquiescence. And apparently he was under-skilled in indifference.

Still.

CHAPTER SEVEN

THE GENTLE SPLASH of a big body moving in the pool was easy to hear even though Brad worked hard to keep it quiet. Sera stood by the closed curtains, thinking. She owed him an apology but the bright light of morning was probably the right time to extend it, right?

Although, he was still up… And she was still up…

And he'd already seen her pyjamas.

She reached between the curtains and quietly unsnicked the lock, then slipped the rest of her body through as she opened the door. Brad hung off the wall at the far end of the pool, staring out into the night, steam from the heated water shimmering up and away into the cold desert air, oblivious to her presence. But when she turned back from closing the door behind her he wasn't oblivious any longer. He twisted, still hanging there in the deep, wordless, his guarded eyes watching her emerge. She took a deep breath and moved to sit on the corner edge of the pool, her feet on the second step. The water's temperature was virtually the same as the warm bed she'd just left, but its wet caress felt gorgeous, like warm silk, and its temperature soaked up to the part of her that was exposed to the winter desert air and warmed her through.

Or maybe that was just the sight of a semi-naked Brad.

'Can't sleep?' he murmured from the other end of the pool. Making nice.

Nope—her mind was too busy. But she just shrugged.

Brad reversed his position, his bent arms spread like powerful angel wings behind him, supporting his body in the deep end so he could face her. It was simultaneously casual and on guard but it did nothing to diminish his strength. If anything, the sheen of the water glistening on all those muscles just amplified their power, making it hard to look away. It was the desert stalking all over again.

Except this time she wasn't lurking in the shadows.

'I wanted to apologise for the silent treatment earlier,' she said, loud enough to be heard above the water cascading over the pool's edge into its collection area, but quiet enough to be personal.

He masked his body language. 'You don't have to be any particular way with me. And you don't owe me any apologies.'

'Because it's your job?' she asked tightly, staring at the water. Or because he didn't care? And why did that make her feel so miserable?

'Because it's none of my business,' he clarified.

That brought her eyes up. 'What if I want to make it your business?'

Those big shoulders shrugged but it was far from easy. 'Then I'll listen.'

Could he sound any more reluctant?

She studied the ripples spreading across the surface of the water from her submerged calves and tried to find a place to start.

'I know it's not reasonable of me to expect you to open up to me on command—like what the deal is with the camel driver—I just feel like…' Her waving hands tried to grasp the words she needed. 'I've trusted you with some of myself—I think I wanted it to be reciprocal. Like…friends.'

God, it sounded pathetic aloud.

'You're a client, Sera,' he said carefully.

One leg kicked out, destroying the pretty water rings on the water's surface. 'I know. I have no right to expect anything more from you than your protection. I just thought getting to know you was a way to be more comfortable around each other.'

His brows dipped. 'I make you uncomfortable?'

'No, not… That sounds worse than I meant it. We have weeks yet together, Brad, and it would be nice not to be on eggshells for that. But I can't be at ease when I know nothing about you.'

And then she might as well be here all alone…

'I've answered your questions.'

Yes, like a good employee. 'You've told me facts. Some. But I don't feel like I know you any better.'

"I'm your responsibility, but not your friend",' he murmured gently. 'That was your ground rule.'

He pushed away from the pool edge and swam out into the middle. Small as it was, that put him much closer to her but he didn't come too close. He just drifted there, sinking up to his nose in the heated water so that only his veiled eyes looked back at her.

'Yes, I did say that.'

'Did you not mean it?'

'I did mean it.' At the time. But somewhere in the past ten days, things had changed.

He surfaced long enough to say, 'So where's the problem?'

Some noise out in the desert drew her eye but

really it was just an excuse to avoid his question long enough to think of the best way of wording her answer.

'Shouldn't I trust you? As my protection? Isn't that important?'

He slowly pushed up out of the water, eyes steady. And concerned. 'You don't trust me?'

'I barely know you. Meanwhile you know all about me. Including things I probably don't even know.' Who knew what else her file had in it? 'It doesn't feel balanced.'

And she was hardly someone who needed barriers to trust.

'So you're looking to even up the score a little?'

'I'm just looking to get to know you, Brad.'

Wary grey eyes pinned her. 'Why?'

His see-all focus made her intensely uncomfortable and snappier than she'd meant to be when she'd come out here with apology on her lips.

'Because we're living in each other's pockets.'

'From what you've said, I'd have thought you'd be used to people maintaining a professional distance.'

A fist squeezed deep down inside and she replied, 'I am. Entirely.'

His big hands paddled him a little closer. Just a little. 'But you don't like it.'

Some questions weren't really questions.

His voice, when he spoke next, was rich with caution. 'You know we can't hook up, right?'

That brought her head up with a whip-crack. She practically reared back. 'I wasn't offering a hook-up. I was just wanting to get to know you a bit.'

Which was starting to feel like a really dumb idea, now.

She pushed up from the edge of the pool, but one powerful stroke had Brad there in time to grab her ankle and tug her gently back down to the tiled edge, now wet with spilled water. Her calf brushed down his smooth chest and tingled the whole way. The spilled water soaked into her behind as she sat back on the pool edge. But she didn't care. She almost didn't notice.

She was all about his hand on her leg.

'Relax, Sera,' he said, releasing her. 'Just a re-minder of protocol. What do you want to know? If I can tell you, I will. Within reason.'

She stared as the umbrage started to drain back out of her. Did she look as wild as her hammering heart suggested? Okay, so maybe coming out here in the middle of the night in her pyjamas wasn't the *least* loaded way she could have done this. But she trusted Brad was above tacky scenarios.

'What is the deal with the camel man? All the secrecy?'

He stared at her, his busy mind turning over. *Really? He couldn't even—?*

'Salim and I don't acknowledge each other in the work context. It's an etiquette thing.'

'He's your friend?'

'He's my uncle,' Brad shot back. Then, as she flared with the surprise, 'Honorary uncle, at least. My mother's cousin.'

Astonishment stole her words for a few moments. Brad was half-Bedouin? 'What's he doing at Al Saqr?'

'His job. He's worked the camels here since the resort opened. It sits on the edge of his tribal lands. He gave me the in with the Sheikh's security team.'

A camel-driver...?

'He must be well regarded. If his recommendation goes that high.'

'Bedouin are not judged by the task they do, but by the men they are. Salim's family is older even than the Sheikh's.'

'And when you're at the resort, you pretend not to know each other?'

He shrugged. 'It's not a secret, but we just don't flash the connection about. Upper management knows, of course. But no one else. Salim's call, and I respect it.'

Sera blinked at him. 'Your mother's cousin. So she's where you get your dark colouring?'

His chest expanded hard, bringing him up out of the water a little, then he sank back down again as he breathed out. 'She grew up just over the border.'

'And so your father's side are Australian?' His half-submerged head nodded. 'And you grew up there but now you live here?'

He emerged from the water, carefully. 'I work here. Like thousands of other ex-pats.'

Immediately, she wondered which he identified as—Aussie or Arabic. 'Away from your family?'

'I have plenty of family here.'

'But your parents...?'

'There's a big wide world out there, Sera. Most people leave home by their twenties...'

She was glad for the soaking her rump was getting on the pool edge because it helped to off-set the flaming heat of her embarrassment. She'd often felt like she lived in a bubble, but how had it never occurred to her simply to *burst* that bubble? Move away.

Was she too unprepared for the real world?

'Your knowledge of Arab culture. That comes from your mother?'

His eyes grew shadowed. 'My mother surrendered much of her culture when she married my father. Her choice. So everything I know—and there's still a lot that I don't—comes from my uncle.'

Something occurred to her. 'That's why you understood Omar so well. Because you were raised just fine outside of your culture, too.'

'I was raised how I was raised. If Mum had practised her culture then I guess I would, too. But she didn't and so I don't. I'm not broken.'

And I don't need fixing. The subtext was clear.

She let some silence flutter down onto the extra heat her questions had caused. Breathing space for both of them.

'I can't tell you what I'd give to know both sides of my family...' She sighed.

His eyes softened and they filled with something that might have been understanding. Or even regret. 'Yeah, I get that. I was nearly adult before I met Salim and his family. I'm treated more like a son there. Instant siblings.'

'I could have brothers and sisters,' she murmured after a long pause, 'and I wouldn't even know it.'

Brad peered up at her. 'If you asked your father would he tell you?'

'He would, I'm sure. But he doesn't know either.' She felt shamed, as always, at the tawdriness of her conception. 'He didn't even know her last name.'

That brought Brad's head up. 'Wait. So he took a tiny baby from a stranger and just trusted that it was his?'

'She acted anonymously through a lawyer. And she sent DNA test results, which he had verified. But he didn't need them. He said I was the spitting image of him as a baby.'

Doubt soaked his face. 'I've seen your father online. I can't imagine you and he looking anything alike.'

'Stage make-up.' She shrugged. 'It's all smoke and mirrors. He can walk down the high street and hardly anyone recognises him. Except as their neighbour. It's kind of cool.'

His eyes narrowed. 'Answer me this, Sera. Is all your agitating an attempt to get his attention?'

Lord, he made her sound as if she were still ten years old.

'My agitating?' She laughed. 'I've marched in a few protests and raised money for causes—'

'And been arrested in a secret research lab. I'm just wondering if you were always so…social-minded.'

She studied him and wondered what he would think of her endless attempts to be exceptional as a child. 'I was a good student, a good worker. I didn't smoke, or drink or party. I studied hard and excelled academically.'

'Not exactly the way to win friends and influence people when you're a teen.'

'I wasn't interested in winning friends. I wanted respect. My teachers, my carers—'

'Your father?'

'Of course.'

'Did it work?'

'Not really. He didn't notice the good girl, but I was too good at heart to be a convincing bad girl.'

'And so the causes.'

She inclined her head. 'I thought it would please him to see that I'd inherited his sense of social justice.'

'And did it?'

'No. I think that was more his thing. His brand. Maybe more of a construct than I realised.'

Certainly, his PR firm were less than happy to see her treading the same path. Stealing focus.

'You know, you're pretty resilient, considering.'

Resilience. Desperation. *Potato...potahto.*

A laugh barked out of her. 'No, I'm not.'

Brad's hand slid onto her foot and just pressed there as though it were her hand.

'You are. More than you think.' He said this with such confidence she almost believed him. 'Or you wouldn't be looking to trust someone again so soon after the whole lab thing.'

'You mean Mark.'

'I'm sorry that happened to you, Sera. You don't deserve it.'

'I walked into it. With my eyes wide shut.'

'You blame yourself.'

'Of course.'

'Getting close to you to leverage your fame was an incredibly low act. It says more about your lousy ex than it does about you. Give yourself points for picking up and carrying on.'

She didn't want his words warming her. And he wouldn't want that either.

'Lying low, I believe you called it.'

'Healing.'

She peered out at the beautiful night. 'If there's a place for that, this is certainly it.'

Brad circulated the water around him gently, keeping it—and the mood—carefully moving.

'So look at us having a regular conversation.' She chuckled.

His smile—so broad and so white against the comparative tan of his skin—lit up the pool. 'Pretty painless, really.'

And just like that, her ability to speak completely dried up. Something about his strong hand on her foot, that twisted smile and those bottomless grey eyes peering up at her from the pool steps… Words completely failed her. Because you needed breath to make sounds, didn't you? The only part of her that could function was her eyes, and those seemed drawn in to his like a tidal current.

Such inscrutable, unfathomable eyes.

Thick lashes rescued her by falling down over Brad's gaze and severing the tractor beam drawing her towards him. His hand slid away from her foot and he pushed against the pool wall and drifted back to the safety of its deep middle.

Back to a professional distance.

'Do you do Christmas?' she blurted without re-alising she was about to.

'Do I *do* it?'

'You know—family, gifts, food.'

'If that constitutes Christmas, then, yeah, I do that. With Dad's side of the family. Not this year, obviously.'

Because he was babysitting her. 'I'm sorry.'

Those big shoulders shrugged. 'I'll call home, video chat. Maybe put on a candy-cane tie to mark the day.' But his eyes narrowed. 'Unless you have other plans for the day?'

'Lord, no.' She shook her head. 'I don't want to impact on your Christmas at all. I've done quite enough of that in my life.'

He studied her through the slight mist rising from the warm pool water. 'What were your Christmases like?'

'Quiet. Unless we had ourselves a bona-fide miracle and Dad made it home. Then it was anything but. He filled the house with his muso friends. It was crazy.'

From one extreme to the other.

Brad's lips thinned. 'So even when he was home your father still managed to ruin your Christmas?'

God, when had she ever laughed about this? But there it was...an actual chuckle. Brad had a gift for easing her worst ouches. Smoothing them over the way his big hands skimmed the water's surface right now.

'What about when he wasn't?'

'I asked for a roster,' she admitted. 'So that no one lost their whole Christmas Day to looking after me. Nanny in the morning. Tutor in the afternoon. Security at night. Same on Boxing Day. It worked well. I got to see just about all of them over the holidays.'

'That's something, I guess.'

'Except that it meant I was taking three people away from their tree or their roast or their *Miracle on 34th Street* so they could sit with me instead. I still didn't like that.'

'Doing to some *other* kid what your father's music did to you?' he murmured.

When had anyone *got* her quite so easily?

But as they stared at each other—as they *got* each other—Brad's eyes lost their warm kind of interest and flattened out. She felt the chill immediately.

'Well, don't worry on my account,' he joked, bringing the conversation back into the shallow end even as he pushed out deeper in the pool. 'I'm just as happy to let this one slide. I'm still working off last year's turkey in the gym.'

Dismissed.

Suddenly, tiptoeing out here to make good on her earlier rudeness looked a whole lot more desperate and intrusive. This might have been her deck during the day, but while he was sleeping out here, it was virtually his bedroom. And she'd let herself into it without knocking. And while he might have been kindly willing to humour her get-to-know-you questions, he was under zero obligation to indulge her swilling hormones.

He cleared his throat. 'Do you think you will be able to sleep now?'

She tucked her wet feet under her on the edge of the pool. 'Yeah, I think so. Thank you for the chat.'

He nodded once—very military, very proper. She missed the Brad of moments ago already. But if nothing else, at least she knew he was in there. Lurking.

She pushed up onto her feet. But as she did, the talc-fine sand that covered everything out here mixed with the pool water into a treacherous slime and she felt her weight-bearing foot slip out from under her. There was no graceful, Hollywood tumble into the waiting water. There was no dramatic cry even. Just the awful, spine-jarring *grunt* as her bottom hit the pool edge, the pain of her tongue caught between her teeth as they slammed shut, and the inelegant face-first slam into the shallow end.

Whereupon she flailed around like a kid who'd never learned to swim, sucking down water, until strong hands wrapped around her and helped her to right herself.

'I've got you...'

Brad pulled her to her feet and steadied her as she spluttered and coughed and pushed the soggy hair out of her face. Spears of pain shot outward from her lower back and, as soon as she had enough breath, she wasted it on a very unlady-like curse. But it was only as she wiped the saline water from her eyes that she glanced down and saw the real humiliation—her flimsy pyjamas glued to her naked breasts like a plaster-cast moulding. She ducked back under the protection of the water with a tiny squeak.

'Are you okay?'

She was still too winded for actual speech so she just nodded and concentrated on taking some shallow breaths. His hands were all over her then, checking her limbs and tipping her head back to examine her pupils. She stood, compliant, under his examination but didn't rise above water level.

'You didn't hit your head?'

She shook her head and nothing rattled so...no.

'Okay, let's get you out.'

She tried to shy back from him but movement under water was slow and it took him a moment to notice her full-bodied resistance. He frowned as she disentangled herself from his arms.

'I can't...' she gasped past her breathlessness, glancing down.

That was when he noticed how transparent her pale blue pyjamas had become, even though she still had everything important carefully obscured under the water. A flood of colour ran up his jaw.

Who knew they even still made men who could blush?

'Okay, hang on, I'll get you a towel.'

He hauled himself up the stairs—and she wasn't so shell-shocked from her tumble that she didn't enjoy the up-close view of that from below—and then he grabbed up one of the oversized guest towels that the resort staff replaced every day, apparently regardless of whether they were used or not. He shook it out and held it up, carefully and strategically, between her see-through PJs and his gaze.

'Come on out. Use the safety rail.'

After her slip of moments ago you bet she would!

She pushed her wobbly legs over to the far edge of the stairs, wrapped her hand securely around the rail and gingerly pulled herself up the four steps to the timber deck. The pain increased with every step out of the zero gravity of the water.

Brad turned slightly to respectfully orient the opened towel in her direction and she walked into it exactly as if she were walking into his arms. And when they closed around her all warm and strong it was like the hug she desperately needed.

He pulled her into his chest, wrapped the towel tight. 'Do you think you've fractured anything?'

It was hard to remember his concern was purely professional as she stood here wrapped in warm towel and wet man, but she managed it, barely.

'I think I've bruised my—' *pride* '—coccyx.' The crack she'd heard on landing on the tiled edge of the pool certainly suggested so.

His hands rubbed her limbs through the towel like a soggy child, and the contact made her feel anything but. He moved out from behind her, holding the towel pinned closed so that she could turn in its circle and grasp its edges together herself and maintain her own modesty.

'Take a quick shower and then I'll take a look.'

'You will not!'

'I need to know if it's fractured, Sera.'

'Unless you have X-ray vision, I don't think you're going to be able to do that by looking.'

His consternation was immediate. 'You're right. I'll call Reception—'

'No!' What was it? Nearly two-thirty a.m.? 'Look, just…come in. We'll sort it out in here.'

She dripped on the tiled floor and the ornate rugs as she crossed into the bathroom. Brad rummaged her up some clothes, and she tried really hard not to wince as big, masculine hands passed her own lacy smalls along with something dry to wear in to her through the bathroom door.

'Be careful.'

'It was just a slip, Brad. I'm not an invalid.'

Though truth be told she really felt like one. The jar on her coccyx was still resonating through her wobbly legs, especially as she bent to peel soggy pyjama bottoms and underwear off. But a hot shower freshened her up a treat, and after, she pulled herself into the T-shirt and leggings that Brad had grabbed for her. Totally mismatched, but that was a man for you. At least they weren't transparent. She combed her towel-dried hair, scrunched it a bit to give it some body and moved towards the door. At the very last moment, she stepped back to smudge some kohl around her lashes and patted on some clear lip gloss.

Just because she *was* a certified disaster zone didn't mean she had to look like one.

Brad shot to his feet from his chair, oblivious to her face, making her efforts as *in vain* as they *were vain*.

He thrust something towards her. 'I made you an ice pack.'

Because that was what you really wanted after a nice hot shower—the block from your minibar freezer. But she took the folded package gratefully and dutifully reached around behind to press it on her lower back.

Her groan was immediate. Yeah. That felt a bit too good. Maybe it was a fracture after all?

'On the bed,' Brad ordered, frowning.

Any other time... The thought made her giggle and he glanced at her with concern as she hoisted herself up gingerly onto the *Princess and the Pea* bed.

'I'm *fine*,' she urged. 'No head injury.'

He helped her to arrange the multitude of pillows and cushions in such a way that she could lie on her side and not on her offended flesh.

'I'm just going to lower your underwear.'

The giggles came back in force.

'I'm serious, Sera.'

'I know, that's what makes it so funny.'

He muttered something under his breath, then, 'I'll laugh when I know you haven't fractured your spine on my watch.'

'It's my bum, Brad. It was built to cope with impact.'

The giggling returned because that sounded way dirtier than she'd meant it—maybe it was a delayed kind of shock, after all—but his serious hands simply rolled her more fully onto her side and relieved her of the ice pack. Then warm fingers tugged her leggings and underwear modestly down and got busy gently pressing on and around the base of her spine.

Could a man ever look you in the eye again after studying your *pants cleavage* close up?

They were about to find out.

His touch was both gentle and a little bit too interesting, and he misinterpreted every flutter of her flesh as pain. Necessarily the inspection took twice as long as it needed to before Brad finally offered his verdict as he eased the ice pack back on.

'I don't think it's fractured.'

'How much experience have you had with busted coccyx?'

'I've assessed other fractures in the service,' he muttered. 'I'm sure the principles are transferable.'

And suddenly her mind was full of military Brad, deep in some awful conflict zone, dirty and sweaty and besieged, urgently doing first aid on a mate covered in blood and broken, shattered limbs. The giggles dried up completely.

'Thanks for checking,' she said, her voice low.

'No problem.' He kept the ice in place with the reliable pressure of his hand, and she gave up her futile attempts not to roll back into the mattress sag where he sat next to her and just let herself relax against the warm heat of his thigh and hip. After the warmth of his enquiring fingers, the cold of the ice was a tantalising contrast.

'Sorry about all of this,' she murmured. Clumsy, clumsy Sera. 'It wasn't intentional.'

The bed shook slightly with his rumbly laugh. 'If I thought it was a ploy to get half-naked in my arms then you'd be the lamest femme fatale ever.'

Suddenly the memory of being in his arms with nothing but a towel and her wet PJs between them returned in full force and she ducked her face to prevent him from spotting her flush. But it wasn't embarrassment causing it. He shifted the pack again and used his fingers on her hips to hold his hand, and the pack, in place. Then he shifted slightly, leaning over her, and retrieved a glass of water from the backlit wall niche above the bed-head.

'Here, take these. It's probably going to get worse before it gets better.'

Generally, she avoided painkillers but something told her he knew a thing or two about injuries. She pushed up onto her elbow to toss the little white pills in and then took a healthy swallow of water to wash them down.

He relieved her of the glass, and she sagged back against his solid strength.

'I'll keep the ice on until you fall asleep,' he murmured. 'Just close your eyes.'

Lord, that was tempting as all his heat soaked into her. 'What if you fall asleep, too?'

'Then the thump of me hitting the ground will wake us both and you can hold an ice pack to my butt instead.'

The idea of holding anything against all that muscle brought a dreamy smile to her face but she was in no mood for conversation. She squirrelled down against him on a happy sigh and let her eyes drift shut. Distantly, very distantly, she felt the heavy heat of his other hand on her head and a moment later the gentle brush of his fingers as he singled out a length of hair and curled it around his fingers, then pulled it out gently.

Over and over.

He probably thought she was asleep. Ten seconds more of this and she would be. Maybe it was the drugs, or the pain—or the excruciating sweetness of the gesture—but she couldn't help the fat tear that squeezed out from under her lashes as she lay there under Brad's gentle touch. But as long as she was turned away from him, she was free to enjoy his secret caress—and indulge her tears—as much as she wanted.

And so she did. Until darkness claimed her.

CHAPTER EIGHT

WITH NO ONE to wake her to go and learn archery or participate in an early-morning wildlife walk or watch the sun rise from a hot-air balloon, Sera slumbered right through dawn, right through the return of their friendly neighbourhood oryx, right through her scheduled dune-drive and right through breakfast.

As soon as she'd nodded off, Brad contacted the resort's night staff to cancel their morning activity and confirm suite delivery for a very late breakfast instead of the restaurant for an early one. Whatever Miss Independence thought she'd be doing today she was in for some disappointment. She was staying in and he was staying with her to make sure she cooperated. He might have finally been persuaded that she hadn't hit her head but even *his* teeth had rattled with the force she'd hit the poolside, spine-first.

Sera was going to be really sore today. She was probably due a down day, anyway. Between her endless photography, array of activities and thorough desert walks, she'd been running on full speed since they arrived. Not exactly R&R.

Though, with what he'd learned about her Christmases past that was starting to make more sense. As was her general uptightness about...pretty much everything. Little Miss Clumsy had ridden her share of rubbish waves in life.

Brad eased his weight from his left leg to his right against the far wall of the suite. He'd only left her for as long as it took to run next door and get some dry clothes at about three a.m. Since then he'd stood guard as far from her bed as he could manage and still do his job. Something about watching her sleep made him feel like a creep— even if he did have good intentions.

If not for him, Sera wouldn't have hurt herself at all. If not for his determination to keep her safe she would have been tucked up in bed comfortably asleep last night instead of zonked out on painkillers.

What was it with him that the more he tried to keep someone safe, the worse it ended up for them?

What he should have done was send her back inside the moment she stepped foot outside her suite. Or made some excuse and left, himself. What he *shouldn't* have done was let himself be drawn into her gentle questions. To convince himself that keeping client relations positive was more important than keeping a professional distance.

Distance existed for a reason.

Had he truly not learned that from Cairo?

'Ow…'

A muffled curse came from under the goose-down quilt. He'd lowered the temperature in her suite to make sure she really snuggled into all those covers, and it had helped her tumble into the very deep slumber that followed. Shambolic hair emerged first and then the squinty eyes gone full panda with the eyeliner she'd put on after her shower.

As if her chocolatey eyes needed the adornment.

'Morning,' he said cheerily, but mostly so that she knew immediately that he was still in the suite. 'I thought you were never going to wake.'

Total lie. He'd sat here in silence, hoping she'd sleep as long as possible. The only reason he'd thrown open the curtains now and let the bright light wake her was because their brunch was arriving in fifteen minutes. And it was almost lunch, really.

She pushed upright and then gasped audibly as she sat on her forgotten injury.

'Here…'

He crossed straight to her and piled her pillows the way he had last night. He'd even found two spares in the cupboard and thrown them on for good measure. But she started fighting him immediately, batting his efforts away with her hands, and rolling unhelpfully where he was trying to engineer a bank of pillows.

'I need to…' One hand waved vaguely at the bathroom.

His job became demolition, then, and he tossed all the barriers to her getting out of bed to the foot of the bed, allowing her to ease onto her feet and inch her way into the next room. The little cry of despair that followed could easily have been about the panda eyes as much as the pain of lowering herself onto the toilet with an injured coccyx and—sure enough—when she emerged a little later her hair was brushed and the smeared eye make-up was wiped clean.

She still looked gorgeous. Just a different kind of gorgeous.

And he wasn't allowed to appreciate either.

Sera frowned at the bright light piercing through a gap in the suite's thick drapes. 'What time is it?'

'Time for brunch,' he said. 'It'll be here any minute.'

She grabbed up her robe and shrugged it carefully on at the discreet knock that sounded at the door. It was their breakfast—with a generous side serve of official guide. Eric looked both unsurprised and unconcerned to find him in here with her.

'I heard about your injury,' he said, walking in behind the room service who got to work immediately setting breakfast out on the deck dining area. 'Are you okay?'

'I will be.' Sera smiled, though it was thin, and Brad guessed she was in dire need of another dose of painkillers.

'Good call cancelling the dune drive today,' Eric said. 'Two hours bumping up and down sand dunes would not have been fun for you. Though the photo ops might have distracted you a little.'

Dark eyes came straight to his in silent thanks, then returned to Eric. 'I hope I can book again. I was looking forward to it.'

'Any time. I'm always happy to go up the big dunes.'

'Thanks for checking up on her,' Brad said when conversation dwindled to awkward silence.

'Actually, I come for another reason.' The vaguely uncomfortable expression on Eric's face piqued both their interest. The first time the unflappable guide had looked anything other than totally in command all week. 'An invitation.'

Instinct stiffened Brad's spine. No, no…

'Who from?' Sera asked, stepping forward.

'Actually…' Eric frowned. 'It's from Salim, your camel driver from last night.'

Sera glanced his way for a heartbeat, just in time to catch his glare. 'Oh? That's…unexpected.'

That was what his uncle had grabbed him to murmur so briefly on the sands last night. A family gathering. But to invite a client… This client…

What the hell was he thinking?

Eric looked as curious extending the invitation as he did uncomfortable.

'Here's the thing…' he said, glancing at the wait staff still setting up breakfast on the deck and lowering his voice further. 'Salim is a good man. He could get in a lot of trouble for this, but an invitation in Bedouin culture is a really big deal. So I promised him I would bring it to you personally. To keep it quiet.'

He stepped forward to hand her a slip of paper with the details on it, but Brad got there first.

'If you wanted to protect him, why didn't you refuse his request? This is against policy.'

Which made the gesture as crazy as it was incomprehensible. Though his uncle never did anything without consideration.

But rather than answer him, Eric turned his gaze back to Sera. 'Salim loves what he does and Al Saqr's guests love the experience he offers—no one would win if he was to be removed from service here. His enormous family least of all.'

'You're asking me to keep it secret?' Sera murmured, glancing his way again.

'I'm…' Eric sighed. 'Yeah, I guess I am. I can tell Reception that you have an activity in Kafr Falaj tonight. I can drive you to Salim's camp and back myself.'

Except that Aqil knew Sera couldn't go outside Al Saqr's fences without deportation. So that would only raise suspicion.

'That won't be necessary,' Brad began. 'Sera's too injured to attend.'

Dark indignation swung his way. 'I'm not too injured to sit in a luxury SUV and then have dinner,' she argued. 'He's hardly going to send camels to collect us.' But then the idea seemed to grab hold of her and she turned back to Eric worriedly. 'Is he?'

Brad tried a different approach. 'You don't know him, Sera—'

Never mind that *he* did…

'That's what dinner invitations are for, Brad,' she said sweetly. 'To get to know people.'

'Bedouin hospitality is second to none,' Eric urged. 'It's how their tribes traditionally gathered information to help them thrive. It's practically in their DNA. It really is an honour to be asked.'

'So we're to be held hostage by cultural niceties?' Brad growled at Eric.

But he knew what was really going on. His uncle had excellent networks within the resort; he must have heard about all the cosy meals he'd been sharing with Sera, the whole sleeping-on-the-deck thing. Obviously, he wanted a legitimate opportunity to check things out for himself.

'Please extend our regrets to—'

'I'd love to accept, Eric. Thank you—'

Brad snapped his gaze to hers. 'Sera…'

'—but I can't leave Al Saqr's grounds, so I must very regretfully decline.'

She looked pleased as Punch to have found a

tidy way through this dilemma. Except it solved nothing.

Eric's face brightened. 'Salim is an elder of the Bani Khalid tribe. Their lands once included these deserts, so he has traditional land rights.'

She turned her confusion to Brad.

'Salim's traditional camp is inside the fences.' He sighed. 'Over on the far boundary.'

'Well, then...' Her smile was both slow and brilliant as she turned to Eric. 'Please tell Salim I would be honoured to attend.'

'Sera—'

'You don't have to come if you don't want to, Brad.'

'My job is to ensure your safety.'

'Good, then.' Her gaze twinkled way too much for someone who was still in pain. 'I'm sure you'll also be very welcome. I'll vouch for you,' she teased.

The service staff returned from the pool deck and nodded to Eric that breakfast was ready to go. Then they took their leave. A few moments later their crowded little suite was quiet again.

'Curiouser and curiouser,' she said, all innocent Alice, limping past him towards breakfast.

'Why did you say yes?' Brad gritted.

She turned back in feigned surprise. 'Because an elder of the Bedouin asked me to dine. And because I'm unlikely to get an opportunity like it ever again.'

'It wouldn't have anything to do with getting to snoop inside my family some more?'

'Gosh, someone has tickets on themselves,' she muttered, just loud enough for him to hear. But her grin gave her completely away.

'Sera—'

'Oh, Brad, relax. You'll be perfectly safe there. An entire tribe to protect you from my rampant curiosity...' She plonked a pillow onto her seat at the outdoor table and eased her bruised spine down onto it.

Relax. As if that were going to be at all possible once Sera was surrounded by his family.

'That's not exactly what I'm worried about,' he gritted.

Though he couldn't begin to tell her what he was truly worried about. That seeing her immersed into his family's life was hardly a good way to toughen his resolve against her.

She lifted her tired eyes to him and they were filled with offence. 'Your secret is safe with me, if that's what you're worried about. Besides, refusing would have to draw more attention than going, don't you think?'

He sighed. 'The Bedu are interconnected, Sera. Everything I do reflects on my uncle and vice versa. I just don't want the lines crossed. I don't like this.'

But Eric was right about one thing. An invitation was a very big deal. Still, first opportunity he got he was going to call his uncle and find out what the hell was going on. Sera had seven hours in which to discover she really was too sore to go. Maybe sense would win out over stubbornness.

And maybe an inland sea would spring up in the desert overnight.

The desert sun sank just after five p.m. at this time of year, but there was more than enough light as Brad drove them into his uncle's compound to showcase the array of traditional camp tents with their tall, woven roofs and open fronts. With the sun low in the west, the shadows cast by the large tent tops matched almost exactly the geometry of the dunes in the distance behind it, like a model version of the real thing. Interspersed with spotless, late-model four-wheel drives.

'Does Salim's family live here?' Sera asked,

craning from her seat to get a better look at the little tent village. 'In the desert?'

'Some Bedouin have fully assimilated into modern culture,' he said, rubbing at the tension in his neck, 'and others have rejected it. My uncle's tribe straddle both sides; they work and earn a living on the fringes of contemporary society but spend every other waking moment out here on their traditional lands. Today was a rest day for my uncle and his brothers so they headed up-country as soon as they were free to. It's where they can breathe,' he finished, almost sadly.

Sure enough, a half-dozen robed and sandalled men with heads comprehensively wrapped in earth-toned fabrics milled around under the biggest of the shelters, while around the camp scuttled dozens upon dozens of boys and girls.

'Ordinarily, Bedouin women over sixteen retreat to a separate tent when strangers come,' he said, guessing the direction of her thoughts, 'but they do come together on special occasions. My uncle understands I cannot let you out of my sight, so tonight the family will mix. It's practically a festival,' he murmured.

Sera couldn't help the instinctive frown.

'Don't feel too sorry for them.' Brad chuckled.

'Aaliyah says the conversation of the men is intensely dull compared to the quality gossip in the women's tent. I doubt they'll be hurrying to emerge, except perhaps to meet you and assuage their curiosity.'

'Aaliyah?'

'My cousin. A bunch of times removed.'

'How many children does your uncle have?' she asked.

'Three daughters and four sons,' he replied.

That brought her eyes back from the camp around them. And a heart-squeeze with it. Who might she be if she'd grown up with that many siblings? That much noise. That much company.

'That's a lot of mouths to feed.'

'Family is everything in Bedouin culture. Bloodlines are fiercely protected.'

Their SUV bumped along the well-worn sand track and finally pulled between dunes into the heart of Salim's tent village. The man himself strode towards them, arms outstretched.

'If anyone gives you anything, take it,' Brad muttered as she undid her seat belt. 'And eat whatever is put before you.'

She flooded with sudden nerves. Of all the timing…!

'Welcome, my friends!'

Salim offered Sera a strong, weathered hand to help her carefully down from the four-wheel drive. He seemed a completely different man from the one who'd wrangled the camels for them a night earlier. Totally commanding.

'I am sorry to hear of your injury. We will make you very comfortable with us.'

'Thank you for inviting me, Salim. I am…honoured.'

Brad saved her from the awkwardness of the clunky formality by jogging around from his side of the four-wheel drive as her feet touched the sands of Salim's camp.

'Welcome also to my home, Mr Kruger.'

'Save your breath, Uncle. She knows.'

Shrewd black eyes swung back her way.

'Does she indeed? Well, that will make things simpler for everyone. I had little confidence in your youngest cousins.' He snorted. 'They can barely keep their *own* secrets…'

Salim turned back to her. 'Come. Meet my family, Miss Blaise.'

'Please, call me Sera…'

It was such a novelty, being the centre of attention, but not because of who she was or who her father was. Dozens of dark, curious eyes watched her every move. And Brad's. Then a stunning young woman in layers of beautiful fabric approached.

'My eldest daughter, Aaliyah,' Salim introduced. 'She will translate for those in my family who do not have such fluent English.'

In the distance, several shorter, rounder women emerged from a side opening in the tent, fully garbed in darkened robes, and hovered towards the back of the gathering crowd, but Aaliyah was spectacularly dressed in layers of the most stunning green and blue fabrics, with a rich veil of the same kind of intricacy as dragonfly wings draped over her dark hair and curled around below her chin. Two generations of Bedouin women looking vastly different—three if you counted the little girls running around in T-shirts and cut-off denim.

Did Salim mourn the changes to his culture or did he accept that they shifted as steadily as the sands all around them?

For a desert people, the skin of their younger women was luminous, and Sera immediately felt self-conscious both for her height and for the comparative plainness of the scarf that she had purchased in the resort's gift shop to drape around her hair.

The next twenty minutes were a crazy barrage of faces and names she would never remember as they inched their way from their vehicle into the main tent. It was closed on two facing sides and open front and back to promote airflow, and huge woven mats laid directly on the sand created a soft, comfortable floor. Five low tables surrounded by cushioned seating filled the space and bunched and tasselled rags lined the welcoming face prettily.

It was all very inviting.

The greatest pile of pillows was reserved for her and her wounded coccyx, and she sank into them gratefully. She'd taken pain relief again in the morning but nothing since then. A fully cloaked woman approached and folded a small pot into her hands with her own surprisingly soft ones murmuring in Arabic as Aaliyah translated.

'My mother wishes that you would use this on your injury. It will ease your pain as you sit here with us this evening.'

Salim's wife clearly had little English but gratitude needed no translation, it seemed, and Sera's effusive gushing got the message across. A few moments of mime told Sera what the woman wanted her to do—rub the unguent directly on her lower back—and Aaliyah and her mother stood more closely together so that she could do it discreetly in the mixed company. Pillows to her back, a human screen to her front.

'*Mukhaddir...*' the mother urged.

Sera opened the fragrant pot, took a quick whiff and then scooped a couple of fingers' worth as though it were commercial chest-rub. Then she reached around under her long shirt where no one could see, snagged her trouser band with her clean fingers and tugged it down to apply the sticky mix directly to the base of her spine. Other than a pleasing, cool tingling, nothing much happened at first, but after only moments she began to feel the full effect as the whole area numbed over.

'It is made from *ruta* and pomegranate pulp,' Aaliyah murmured as Sera sighed with relief. 'My family uses only natural medicines and foods. The land gives us everything we need.'

The talent it must take to find much of anything in these sandy mountains...

'Please, thank your mother. I'm so grateful.'

She glanced around for Brad and found him surrounded by the male members of Salim's family, who were all chatting at a pace. But he caught her eye and started easing his way back towards her, strain easy to see in the tautness of his carefully neutral smile. The stiffness of his posture.

Was he still worried for her safety? Even here amongst his own family?

'Are you okay?' she murmured, leaning briefly towards him as he accepted Salim's invitation to sit and sank down onto the cushions next to her. Immediately people rushed forward with timber platters covered in fragrant, earthy morsels and a big goblet filled with fresh juice.

'I'm fine,' he lied.

Guilt immediately washed over her that she'd forced his hand in coming tonight. Insinuated herself into a part of his life she had no fair right to. Somewhat disguised between the cushions, she stretched her little finger out and brushed it against his in apology. He snatched his hand back reflexively.

Sera straightened and disguised her flush by focusing on Aaliyah's efforts to recall the lingering children into another tent for the evening. But when Salim merely raised his eyebrows in their general direction they all scattered like sand beetles and disappeared behind the intricate weaves. From where they sat, Sera had an excellent view out of the open front of the tent over the golden desert as the sun cast its last light over the sands and it did not take long to soothe the wounded pride out of her.

As soon as the sun vanished, a dozen braziers replaced its warmth inside the tent and fragrant torches were lit outside, and one of Salim's family began to pluck away at a gorgeously carved stringed instrument. The authentic desert music made the perfect backdrop for their conversation. Aaliyah translated all Sera's questions and her family's answers, and made sure she knew what each dish contained as they came out. A cinnamony camel's milk entrée, meat dishes of lamb and antelope, and a constantly refreshed supply of aromatic coffee spiced with cardamom.

'My family are horse and camel-breeders, primarily,' Brad explained next to her. 'That's how they make their staple living. Salim is well known for his talent with difficult horses.'

'You must ride one of my Arabs in the big sands,' Salim announced loudly. 'I will pick you one personally.'

She glanced at Brad, who watched her intently, and suddenly felt the weight of any social slights she might accidentally make. She didn't want to damage the obvious rapport between uncle and nephew.

'I would like that.' Sera smiled. 'As soon as I can sit without wincing. Perhaps you have one that is gentle and patient.'

'We will find one that is also beautiful and courageous. Like its rider.' Salim had the same impenetrable poker face of his nephew and he turned it on him now. 'Do you think that would suit, Bradley?'

Brad looked completely lost for words at his uncle's happy manipulation. Though, he managed one word, at least…

'Certainly.'

Sera sagged back against her cushions, perplexed by Brad's reluctance to pay her any kind of compliment, but more entertained by the obvious mischief in Salim's eyes. Since he wasn't expending it on her. Was it wrong to share this little bit of sport at Brad's expense?

The next half-hour degenerated into a fast and engaging discussion between the men on the relative virtues of four-wheel drives generally and their various models specifically. Then there was a raucous tour outside to the cluster of near-new vehicles parked there including Al Saqr's top of the range SUV.

'The way to a man's heart is through his vehicle,' Aaliyah said as they watched the men go. 'Once, it was camels that were so greatly prized. When our lives depended on them and not on machines.'

The thought of getting caught out on the sands without one ship of the desert or another definitely did not appeal. The sand and sun could suck you dry of all your moisture in a day and leave you no more than a desiccated husk.

The men returned, yet more food was served— this time a delicious meat wrapped in flatbread half-leavened in the ashes of the fire—and loud conversation resumed. Much of it was in the language of the Bedouin and although Aaliyah did her best to keep up she eventually resorted to simply translating the parts that were directed at or about their guests. That gave Sera a chance to breathe. And to just listen. Vigorous argument, cracks of laughter, teasing. She relaxed back against the cushions and enjoyed the energetic vibe.

'Your family are amazing,' she said. 'I've never been to anything like this. There's so much...'

Affection. Intimacy. Love.

'Food?' Brad volunteered, coaxing a laugh out of her.

And as he did, yet more courses were thrust their way—fresh, delicious and mysterious. Sera stopped wondering what was in each dish and just leapt, bruised coccyx and all, into the full cultural experience. She trusted Brad to stop her from eating something she would regret.

Trust.

The thought took her by surprise but, yes, there it was. Actual, earned trust. With her safety, with her diet, and with her bruised bones. She might not know a whole lot about Brad Kruger but some time in the past twenty-four hours it had sprung up between them.

On her side, at least.

'What is this one?' she murmured to Brad as yet another dish was laid before them.

'Lightning,' he murmured.

She turned her confusion to him.

'It's *fagah*. A kind of desert truffle. It is said they form during electrical storms wherever lightning strikes. The electricity changes the very nature of the air and sand and *fagah* are born. The greater the number or severity of desert storms, the greater the resulting harvest.'

It was impossible not to be seduced by his low voice and evocative words.

'Children get intensely competitive hunting for the biggest ones,' he went on, leaning closer into her to be heard over the noise of conversation, 'searching for the telltale fissures in the sand and digging madly to uncover the dessert gem below. In serving *fagah*, the Bedu capture the very lightning to gift it to their honoured guests.'

His words were as close as she'd ever come to the visual richness she experienced in photography. In fact, his vivid descriptions *became* images in her mind, and she longed to go and dig through the sands herself.

And to stay out here forever.

'Beautiful legend,' she murmured as she raised her fork. 'And beautiful food.'

His gaze touched on her like heat. And stayed there. 'So much of this culture is beauty.'

Around them, a passionate discussion sprang up over what had caused more ruin to the Arabian peninsula—the coming of oil, the coming of water or the coming of tourism. Salim eventually murmured to Aaliyah, who stood gracefully and moved to the rear of the tent where another woman met her. Together, they sat on the rugged floor beside the musician as an adolescent boy came out to join him with a piped instrument. What followed was a beautiful four-part song—string, wind and two voices—that needed no translation to hold Sera enraptured.

Afterwards, a less weathered version of Salim stood on his left and began to speak in Bedu, deep and resonant. Without Aaliyah at her side, the words went untranslated but the cadence of the man's speech made Sera think it must be a traditional poem. She let herself sink into his rich tones regardless of her comprehension.

More music followed. Then more stories. Aaliyah returned as Salim himself stood and told a tale in his native tongue. Celebrating the long history of his tribe and how the Arabian deserts were the true homelands of the Bedouin. How they migrated between scarcely fertile areas then moved on and left them to replenish only to return years later. It wasn't hard to imagine this very feast happening out in the middle of the expansive desert. Except perhaps then the dining would have been more meagre. A desert culture was all very romantic until you remembered how close to starving the original Bedouin perpetually were.

Brad gently touched Aaliyah on the hand and

took over the responsibility for translating, bending low and close to her ear so she could hear him without disturbing Salim's oratory.

'He's talking about the Bedouin honour code now,' Brad breathed against her ear, causing tiny flutters up her neck. 'It's the basis for their entire social and justice system.'

Sera glanced sideways to watch Brad, whose eyes were on his uncle as he continued. There was respect there, and affection. It glowed rich in his dark eyes. It wasn't hard from there to let her eyes wander over the strong lines of his bearded jaw, over his lips...

'Me against my brothers,' he murmured as Salim postured grandly, clapping his actual brothers on their shoulders. *'My brothers and I against my cousins, but my cousins and I against strangers.'*

Everyone present cheered, and Brad turned back to her and whispered, 'Family is all to the Bedu.'

Then, in a very determined way, Salim turned to Brad and muttered a few more words directly to him.

Ibn 'amm.

Brad pushed to his feet and clasped Salim's right forearm with his left one. The gesture was at once incredibly masculine yet rich with affection.

Sera leaned across to whisper to Aaliyah, 'What did he say?'

'*Ibn 'amm* means "son of my uncles". He is acknowledging Brad as family.'

'Hadn't he already?'

'Yes, but *ibn 'amm* is more…intimate. He is acknowledging Brad as a kind of son. A son of the Bedu. As my brother.'

Brad's eyes glittered with emotion as the fierce gesture became a manly kind of hug. Everyone around them cheered again. But Sera couldn't join them.

She would never know this much love. This much belonging.

The ache in her heart swelled out through her whole chest.

The shisha came out and the tent filled with the aromatic pleasure of apple-scented tobacco. Right behind that were final coffees. As aromatic and lovely as both were, Sera's enthusiasm for the night had evaporated when Brad had stood and walked to his uncle.

Salim's cue was subtle enough that she completely missed it but everyone else seemed to understand the exact moment the evening was over. Brad helped her gingerly to her feet and suddenly it was all farewells. Sera clung to her little pot of unguent and then found herself loaded down with items to take back to the resort. Some still-warm bread wrapped in plain cloth, a mat woven in the same style as those in the tents, and—from Aaliyah—her scarf.

It was the one thing she baulked at. Even remembering Brad's warning, and even here where beautiful fabrics were so common—such a scarf was too, too precious.

'The only thing that brings the Bedu more pleasure than having a beautiful thing is to gift it to someone else,' Aaliyah assured Sera, unravelling the scarf from her head, pushing it firmly into her hands and folding her fingers over them. 'Sharing our pleasures and hospitality is our greatest pride.'

And then they were off bumping back across the dunes—like Alice scrabbling back up the rabbit hole, or Dorothy waking from Oz—though the road seemed invisible to her in the moonlight. She sagged into the comfortable passenger seat of the SUV and tried to ignore the occasional brush of Brad's knuckles on her leg as he changed gears in the sands.

'Such an extraordinary evening,' she murmured when the comparative silence of the SUV grew too oppressive. Suddenly she had an inkling of how suffocated the Bedouin might feel within the walls of a conventional house. How was she going to eat at a regular table ever again? 'Nothing like I was expecting.'

'What were you expecting?'

Who knew? She couldn't imagine him in any other setting now.

'Your uncle is quite the politician.' She chuckled.

'It is an insult to direct a command to a Bedouin,' Brad murmured, 'so Salim has learned to lead through a careful balance of diplomacy and generosity. He has earned the respect of his people.'

'And his nephew.'

'It is hard not to. He is progressive despite the simplicity of his culture. He believes his children are as much tools of his trade as his animals and sees no reason to let half his tools go blunt by not educating his daughters. Aaliyah is a good example of the wisdom of Salim's approach. She's inherited her father's gifts with horses. Her beauty and her brains will set her in good stead.'

'Good genes obviously run in the family.'

She'd hoped the compliment to earn her a wry smile but it only added an extra line to the fork between his brows.

'Thank you for taking me, Brad,' she said to stop the lingering warmth between them from haemorrhaging out of the vehicle like oxygen from a vacuum. 'It was eye-opening.'

And thought provoking. And it made it a whole lot harder for her to *meep* about her youth when she saw how other young girls were living theirs in this world. They just…got on with it. They accepted the kind of responsibilities they had to their families and let their ambitions align with it. There was a certain desert pragmatism in that that she really liked.

'I didn't *take* you, Sera,' Brad said carefully. 'It wasn't a date.'

Fierce heat flooded her cheeks. 'No, I know that. But you allowed it.'

'The invitation was for you. It wasn't up to me to allow or disallow anything. I'm not your keeper either.'

She turned to face him and spoke carefully. Why was he forcing such distance between them all of a sudden? 'No, you're not.'

His eyes didn't stray off the road ahead once.

'Brad, what's going on? You've been weird since Eric gave me Salim's invitation.'

'Nothing's going on.'

'You were tense tonight. And it can't have been the company.' He must have had dozens of such nights in his years in Umm Khoreem.

But she caught the sideways flick of Brad's eyes. Towards her.

Oh... Unless it *was* the company.

'You're still angry that I accepted?'

'I'm not angry, Sera.'

'Then what—?'

'They are my *family*,' he burst out. 'You invited yourself right into my family. Without a second thought.'

Defence came naturally to her. 'I didn't invite myself, your uncle invited me. If you didn't want me to go you should have said.'

'I'm pretty sure I did say.'

Guilt rushed up under her collar. 'You're reacting like I'm some kind of stalker,' she sputtered. 'It was a dinner invitation, Brad. That's it.'

'It's my family, Sera. You couldn't really have inveigled yourself any deeper in my personal business.'

Inveigled. That was a pretty horrible way of putting it.

'I get that Bedouin propriety means you couldn't

order your uncle not to invite me, but it's hardly my fault that he did.'

'You accepted. Even knowing I wanted to keep professional boundaries between us.'

'Oh, please… What is it that you imagine I'm going to do with this new-found intimacy, Brad? Force myself on you?'

Something ground visibly high in his jaw. 'I'm a professional, Sera. I don't get involved with clients.'

'So you keep saying.' Ad nauseam. 'I'm beginning to wonder who you're trying to convince.'

His lips pressed shut and his eyes remained firmly glued to the road ahead.

Conversation over.

Sera turned to study the dark desert outside the passenger window as humiliation swilled through her. She'd just wanted a chance to see the culture up close, when it wasn't on professional show for guests of the resort. And it would have been rude not to accept.

At least, that was what she'd told herself, but Brad's words sat like a heavy meal in her gut. Dense and uncomfortable.

Was she so eager to belong somewhere—to

someone—that she had insinuated herself right into his world?

It was hardly a flattering image.

'Just take me home,' she murmured, leaning her hot cheek into the cool leather and staring miserably out at the beauty of the desert at night.

Home.

Funny how that could be a country so far from her own. A resort. A suite.

Or a person.

CHAPTER NINE

BRAD PULLED IN to Al Saqr's vast welcome drive-way and leaped out to open her door—because he was paid to, certainly, not because he wished to extend her any kind of courtesy—but her feet found the dark ground well ahead of him.

'I'd like to walk back to the suite,' she said to the night air, not waiting for a response. Or the courtesy buggy. She set off in the direction of home, limping hard and fast.

Brad assumed his usual position—behind her and to her left, a dark shadow in the night. Business as usual, despite the fact they'd sat together and talked and laughed and shared something special this evening.

For her anyway. Maybe nights like tonight were ten a penny to him.

She marched down the gently lit path, ignoring the pleasant night air, wishing she were still ensconced amid cushions and romantic tales and the delicious smell of apple tobacco instead of stumbling awkwardly ahead of a man who believed her to be trying to wheedle herself into his world.

Like some kind of sad cuckoo shoving its way into a nest.

When they arrived at her suite, Brad cleared it silently and then stood back to let her in. The whole room glowed with the gentle light the night staff had left on after preparing her room for the evening. None of the overhead lights were on, only those few built into the wall niches and designed to showcase the interesting artefacts standing in them. The pale colour of the closed drapes reflected the low light around the room while its fabric made the whole place cosy and warm.

And incredibly romantic.

Which only made the sting of the earlier conversation more profound. Would he blame her for this, too? Suspect her of setting some kind of seduction scene?

Silent awkwardness soaked the room like the rich, spreading light.

'I might have my coffee in the pool,' she said just for something—anything—to change the subject. 'My back could use a warm soak.'

He offered no opinion, and no argument. Like a good little bodyguard. 'I'll be right back, then.'

Sera loaded the coffee machine with fresh-ground local coffee and set it to run before padding to the bathroom and changing into her swimsuit. When she emerged on the back deck, steaming coffee in hand, Brad was already there—changed into board shorts and a T-shirt.

'That's going to be chilly tonight,' she commented, glancing at him.

For no reason, she grew instantly self-conscious about his presence. He'd seen her in the pool plenty of times and climbing out of it a few. He'd even *carried* her out of it a dozen short hours ago, but this was the first time she'd had to disrobe in front of him, even if that only meant shrugging out of her wrap. Suddenly the simple act turned into some kind of dance of the seven veils.

Would he accuse her of doing it too provocatively?

'I don't think you have to sleep out here any more, Brad,' she started as he laid out his stuff on the deck lounger he'd been calling his bed. 'I'm not going to go on any more midnight expeditions without letting you know first. I've learned my lesson.'

And she was tired of the energy it took to be around him so relentlessly.

'It's not about that any more,' he murmured. 'I can just be more responsive from here.'

She dipped a toe into the water to test its temperature, stalling terribly. It was nice and toasty against the cold night air. 'What is it you imagine you're going to need to respond to? Murderous plots? Attempts to abscond? Surely I've earned a little faith by now?'

What the hell did she have to do in this world to earn the respect of men like Brad? Or her father?

'I'm good out here,' he said with some finality, perching on the end of the deck lounger and watching her.

Except that she was good at last words, too. 'And if I insisted? If I *ordered* you to go back to your own suite?'

'I might grow suspicious as to why you were trying so hard to get rid of your protection. And then I wouldn't be doing my job if I left.'

Your stupid job, she said in her head. Aloud, she just muttered, 'Whatever.'

She failed miserably at removing her wrap in an unconcerned way and felt as if she'd only managed to draw *more* attention to herself as she peeled it off and let the long fabric pool onto the deck.

Lamest striptease ever.

She was up to her neck in warm water when she heard him wade in behind her.

'If you go A over T again you could do more than just bruise a few muscles,' he said when she turned to gape at him. He settled himself comfortably on the pool's lowest step, a respectful distance from her.

Being treated like a child had always grated. When she *was* a child it was because people expressed their professional care and concern that way rather than in the good old-fashioned way— loving her. And as an adult... Well, no one liked to be patronised.

'I think I can manage to float in the pool without incident, Brad,' she gritted past her suddenly tight chest. Being angry at him wasn't going to be helped by all that bare, hard flesh.

He shrugged his broad, wet shoulders, and she tried not to dwell on how the water streamed down them. 'I'm in, now.'

She rested both elbows on the infinity edge of the pool so her spine hung straight and flat, and the deep water supported her as she stretched out her sore muscles. Her fingers stroked the tiles of the infinity edge as though it were Brad's olive skin. Smooth and just as soothing.

'If you're staying, then I want to talk about to-night,' she said, half back over her shoulder.

That should get him running.

Somewhere in the distance a bird shrieked into the night.

'I don't particularly feel like doing a post-mortem on the evening,' Brad finally said. 'But if it's still bothering you go ahead and commence the inquisition.'

That was man code for back off. So, naturally, she stepped forward.

Or turned, in her case. Hanging from stretched arms along the far edge of the pool.

'Of course it's bothering me. You implied that I was some kind of stalker simply because I accepted your uncle's invitation. Like I'd coerced my way into your life on purpose.'

'Didn't you?'

'I didn't go because it was your family, Brad. I would have enjoyed it just as much if it was Aqil's family. Or anyone else's.'

'It wasn't theirs, it was mine.'

Sadness washed through her. 'I thought we'd become friends enough these past few weeks to give each other the benefit of the doubt, at least.'

'We're not friends, Sera. It doesn't work that way.'

'It was working just fine from my point of view.'

'For me, then,' he said, pushing to his feet and stepping towards the pool's middle. 'Is that what you want me to say? It isn't working for me. It's distracting me from my job.'

'How? Nothing has happened. You're doing your job just fine.' Too diligently, at times.

His brows folded down. 'I've seen it before, Sera. Affection is...an emotional distraction. I don't need the complication.'

Before? He'd been in this situation once before?

'A complication?' she challenged, trying hard not to be jealous about whoever it was that earned his affection in the past. Apparently, *they* were good enough to bend the rules for.

'Honey, you are nothing but complicated.'

A tease of hope burst through her. That didn't sound like the words of a man who was *un*affected. She pushed off the pool edge and stroked towards him.

Immediately, his eyes grew wary.

'Tell me about her,' she said as her feet found the tiles on the pool bottom.

'Who?'

'Whoever you got involved with before. Did it end badly?'

Caution closed his face. 'Really? You're wanting into my personal life again?'

'I just want to understand you.'

He rolled his eyes heavenward but it wasn't irritation. He was searching for something. An escape, maybe? 'Why can't you just step back and let me do my job? Why can't you just be a normal, respectful client?'

'I don't really *do* normal, Brad. I thought we'd established that.' His gaze steadied and locked on her. Full of defiance. She drifted forwards again. 'So who was she?'

Impatience singed his tone. 'There was no "she".'

'A "he" then?' She grinned. 'Go you!'

But his grey eyes weren't the slightest bit amused and their seriousness stopped her in her watery tracks. 'Wait… Really? A he?'

Wow. She'd not seen that coming.

'A child,' he was fast to correct. 'Matteo. The seven-year-old son of a diplomat family I was assigned to in Egypt. He and I became friends. A big-brother kind of deal. He looked up to me.'

As any kid would. Strong and brave and exceptional. What was not to love?

She stumbled over the word even though it was

only a thought. No one needed to be thinking about *love*…

'What happened?' she asked instead.

'He got hurt. Because I was off my game.'

'Did you miss something?' Hard to imagine. He was so thorough.

'No.' His gaze shadowed over. 'Both his parents were embassy staff, with a contingent of diplomatic security as well. That meant I reverted by default to Matteo's cover most of the time. When he was at school. Out playing. Everywhere.'

'That's a lot of together time.'

He nodded. 'Attachment is always a risk with close contact. He was a good kid. He had a bit of hero-worship going on.'

The affection in his gaze—despite being mingled with pain—made it easy to imagine Brad as the father.

Whoa. She pushed that little piece of deluded thinking aside.

'You're referring to him in the past tense,' she said instead.

'When the unrest got too bad, the UN pulled their diplomats out. But not their forces. We stayed behind to defend the evacuated compounds and facilities.'

'So you had to say goodbye to Matteo?'

'I didn't know how hard he had bonded. When it came time to bug out he just…wouldn't go. He wouldn't leave me behind in danger and my orders prevented me from going with them.' His big body sagged. 'He ran off to prevent the car from leaving. As the rebels were swarming towards the embassy.'

'Oh, Brad…'

He knew where her mind had just gone and was fast to correct her. 'No. I found him. But I had to manhandle him into the SUV. Force him in, screaming. I hurt him, Sera. It was…'

Bad enough, apparently, that he couldn't find a word for it.

'But he made it, yes?' She held her breath. *Please say yes.*

He cleared his throat. 'Sixty seconds longer and he wouldn't have. The shooting started. It was a week before I got confirmation that the whole family had made it out.'

What a week that must have been. Wondering… Fearing.

'I thought I'd gotten them all killed,' he gritted.

'But you didn't.'

He took a moment to control his choppy breathing. Then another.

'It doesn't matter. I learned my lesson that day. The rules exist for a good reason, Sera.'

He stood in the shallow end, rolling his hands in and out of the warm water in a figure-eight, letting the rising steam brush across his skin. It reminded her of the way he'd stroked her hair until she'd fallen asleep last night.

Total contrast to Brad, the tough guy.

'I doubt Matteo would agree with you on that point,' she risked saying. 'I was raised by the book, Brad. It's a pretty lonely way to grow up.'

His frown deepened. 'Sera, just because they kept a professional distance didn't meant they didn't care for you.'

'People can't just opt out of their feelings.' God, how much difference would that have made to her childhood if it were true?

'They can opt out of *showing* it,' he bit out. 'If someone is not theirs to care for.'

Silence settled amongst the mist on the surface of the pool.

'Are you wishing that's what you'd done with Matteo?' she finally murmured, stepping towards him far more gently than her hammering heart demanded. 'Or are you saying that's what you're doing with me?'

He backed away two paces. She felt each foot-fall as if it were landing on her ribs and not on the bottom of the pool. Story of her life, really…

'Let it go, Sera.'

Did he have no idea how difficult this was for her? To expose herself like this?

'I don't see you climbing out of this pool,' she pointed out on a deep breath. Could he hear the thrum of her heartbeat in it?

Another backward step. Another slam against her chest.

'My job—'

'Is to stand up there in the corner of the deck and watch our environment,' she interrupted. 'Yet here you are, in the pool—' she swallowed '—watching me.'

A dark flush chased above the waterline. 'That's easily fixed.'

But before he could move she cornered him in the shallows, blocking his exit with her body. And like any desert creature, he didn't respond well to being cornered.

'You're not really one to take no for an answer, are you, Sera?'

She held her ground, though every part of her quailed. Some instinct pushed her onward. An instinct she normally ignored.

'Or are you just trying to show everyone in your childhood how wrong they were?'

That knocked her focus. 'What do you mean?'

'That you were worthy of their affection all along.'

A pulse hammered in her throat but it only seemed to flush her blood away from her face. 'Are you saying I'm not?'

'I…' He sighed, trapped in his own desperate scrabble. 'No, that's not what I'm saying. Of course you're worthy of it.'

Her gut clamped down. 'But just not worthy of you?'

'I'm nothing special, trust me.'

Au contraire. 'You think I'm just looking to exorcise a bit of childhood angst by flirting with you?'

Though, really, they were so far beyond flirting…

'I think you need to be honest about what it is that you're proposing here.'

'Do I really need to explain it?'

He'd run out of pool to back into, and she slid her

arms up around his slick shoulders and used his own strength to hoist herself up closer to his lips. His Adam's apple practically danced beneath the prickle of dark beard that grew down his tanned throat.

'Do I really need to explain how tired I've grown of fighting the thing that zings around between us?' she murmured.

'Sera—'

'Or how I don't think I've ever felt a connection like this with anyone else…ever? Is that the kind of honest disclosure you are recommending?'

She breathed against his mouth, conscious of every place her long, wet body melded into his warm, hard one. She pressed her lips against the corner of his mouth even as he stood like a stone pillar, completely non-responsive. His mouth tasted of salt water and defiance. Though his lips were lusciously full and soft.

'Do you have any idea how hard it is for me to lay myself open like this? Like a skeleton out in those dunes?' She peered up into his dark eyes. 'Or how it hurts to see you stumbling back away from me?'

Regret blazed across his gaze, but she was not about to accept his pity. She hung there—lifeless—

for a moment longer, then used his bare chest to push herself off him and back into the water.

'If one of us has to have a good honest look at their motivations,' she said as she turned away from him towards the steps, 'I don't think it's me.'

'Stop!'

No. She was through hearing his greeting-card thoughts on what she needed to do.

Or be.

Her foot found the middle step, but before she could haul the rest of her sore body up onto it, strong arms banded around her waist and pulled her back into the pool. Like a zero-gravity tango-dip. Water sloshed around her hair and face but Brad wasn't about to let her sink. Besides, you had to swallow water to drown and her lips were too sealed by the astonishing press of his for that to happen. They were firm and whisker-sharp, not a particularly good fit, but even someone as kiss-deficient as she was didn't want an angry—or, worse, *a pity*—kiss.

Both heels of her palms pushed against the slick curve of his shoulders to set herself upright, but he didn't let her go.

'I wasn't backing away to stop *you*, Sera,' he vowed, low, helping her find the pool bottom. But when she did, he still didn't release her. 'I was backing away to stop *me*.'

Helium seemed to fill her body, taking away her pain, even her weight.

'I was stopping for both of us,' she reminded him. 'I was getting out of the pool.'

His grave face pinched. 'I know.'

And then his head dipped towards her again and this time his lips fitted perfectly, they moved perfectly. They stole her breath and thickened her blood *perfectly*. Even the rasp of his trim beard teased her flesh enticingly. Whether from the tight curl of his wet arms around her, the glorious heat and taste of his mouth against her cold flesh, or the sheer shock and exultation of his endless kiss, Sera started to see dark shapes on the edges of her vision. She pulled free and gasped in a life-preserving breath. Then she rejoined him the moment her lungs were replenished. His hands forked up through her dripping hair, holding her face still for the welcome assault of his mouth. She stretched up into his hold, held buoyant by the water, pressing her whole body against his—participating fully, imagining what it was going to be like to tumble together into that massive, cloud-like bed inside and feel his wet weight on top of her.

What it was going to *be* like.

His chest rose and fell with every tortured breath. Eventually he pulled free enough to speak.

'You are an intelligent, creative, beautiful woman,' he murmured against her flesh, and her soul sang almost as much as her skin. But then he set her a little back from him and the sudden distance got her immediate attention. 'And this is one hundred per cent my loss.'

Wait...what?

It took a second for his words to make sense, but while she was still frowning, he hammered his point home by setting her away from him. Well away.

'Go inside, Sera.'

Alone...?

Then it dawned on her what was happening. He'd kissed her. But only for a moment, and now the moment was over. He was already retreating back behind the safe pages of that flippin' book of his. It was like last night's hair stroking—something he did before thinking better of it.

Every rejection she'd ever felt as a kid bubbled back up from the depths where she'd shoved them. She wanted to argue. She wanted to beg. Or scream. Or cajole. But, no, she'd had her fill of being delightful and entertaining and trying to win some hint of genuine affection from the adults around her as she'd grown up. She wasn't about to demean herself now.

She'd already done a good enough job of that by climbing up him like a rat in a flood.

She shrank back from his roasting, cautious regard and forced her heart into that lead-plated place she kept deep inside especially for it.

'Like I said, Brad, maybe it's time for you to go back to your own place at night. I give you my word I won't leave the suite.'

'Sera, listen—'

She crossed her arms over her chest, suddenly cold despite the warm pool water. 'I'm instructing you, as your client, to return to your own suite from now on. Since your professional obligation means so much to you I know you'll comply. Or do I need to call your superiors and get them to instruct you for me?'

A dozen emotions chased behind his eyes—grief, regret, loss, confusion—and finally settled on determination. He was, above all else, a pro.

'Will you be okay?'

Have you broken me for good, you mean?

'You think this is my first rodeo?' she scoffed,

though the effort cost her every bit of strength she had left. She'd faced moments like these all through her life. When she'd tried to get close. When she'd been rebuffed... 'If there's one thing I do know how to do it's a fast rebound.'

She pulled herself out of the water, threw her wrap around her shoulders and went to walk into her suite, still dripping. Gorgeous rugs be damned. She needed to be away from Brad, his opinions, and his pity right now.

Before she truly shamed herself.

As soon as the door and thick curtains were secured behind her, she let the soggy wrap fall to the floor and crossed straight to the bathroom, her trembling fingers pressed against her still-tingling lips. There she climbed into the expansive shower, cranked it up to scalding, and stood under it until all the chills had burned away.

The cascading water disguised her humiliated tears and when her sobs grew too loud, she shoved the saturated washcloth into her mouth to muffle it in case the sounds drifted on the silent desert night to the man in the suite next door.

CHAPTER TEN

AL SAQR'S SUV convoy teetered right at the top of a mountainous dune—the biggest as far as the eye could see outside the protected area—as the rising sun threw spectacular light across the entire desert. Easily the most stunning views Brad had ever seen.

Sera should have been enraptured. And her camera should have been out the whole time, clicking itself into an overheated frenzy.

Eric had worked his guts out trying to give her a quality four-wheel-driving experience, but no matter how much the vehicle tilted or how high he took her or how astonishing the vista, Sera barely even raised a brow. Brad couldn't actually see that for himself from where he was in the back seat, but he could tell from the way Eric kept glancing at her in the front and upping the scare stakes, trying to create some impact.

And from the way Eric glanced back at him a few times in the mirror, he was clearly concerned.

Yeah. He'd been concerned, too, but Sera wasn't about to accept that from either of them.

When the three-vehicle convoy finally climbed its way to the top of the highest dune for miles and stopped there for a thirty-minute exploration break, she at least took a half-hearted photo—with her phone. And that was almost worse than not taking a photo at all. Her expensive gear sat untouched in the bag in the front of the SUV.

She should have been all over this opportunity. Or maybe she should have cancelled again. Despite her injury being a day better now. The dunes lay out before them like a long, serpentine spine running all the way to the horizon but that wasn't what Sera was looking at. She only had eyes for one thing. A tiny, solitary Ghaf tree, far below them, at the bottom of this massive dune; a distant speck of green against all that golden blonde sand. Like some kind of lonely bonsai.

'Can I walk down there?' she asked as Eric stepped up next to her, nodding at the Lilliputian tree.

Eric looked to him for permission and he gave the slightest toss of his chin.

'If you follow the ridge down,' Eric told her, 'and then stay in the shade. We'll pick you up on the way down. Careful!' he added as she set off towards the dune's edge. 'It's steeper and farther than it looks.'

Brad immediately fell in behind her, and she stopped him with a firm, resolute hand. But no eye contact.

'I'll see you at the bottom,' she ordered.

He was probably supposed to argue. This was raw desert, full of scorpions and vipers and random sand monsters. But right now *he* was the most clear and present danger to Sera's well-being. So he let her go, and she started stumbling down the dune face.

'If your back gets too sore just raise your arms,' he called after her. Just as swimmers did in the oceans, back home. 'We'll come and get you in the SUV.'

If she heard him she didn't show it, as disturbed sand cascaded ahead of her. He wondered then if giant dunes could have avalanches.

'Start the vehicle,' he ordered Eric as soon as she was out of earshot, 'and if something happens we're going straight down this hill, nose-first. Be ready.'

Eric did as asked and Brad moved to the sharp edge of the dune and locked his eyes on Sera as she picked her way down the vast mountain of sand. He started to sweat a treat standing there, hatless, under the rising sun. Even in winter and even in the morning it still had bite. It took Sera forever to get down, and she got tinier and tinier, reinforcing just how high above the world they were, until finally she reached that desolate tree and sank down against its trunk.

The image was as heartbreaking as it was striking.

Tiny woman against massive world. And very definitely against him.

Being at odds with Sera didn't sit comfortably. At all.

But he only had himself to blame.

The universe had given him heaps of opportunities to do things differently with her. He could have let the authorities deport her back to London after the plane incident. He could have manned up and rebuffed her very first efforts at friendship. Worked harder to maintain professional distance every day since then. He could have stood in the shadows for every one of her meals and taken the same back seat he took today on every one of her activities. He could never have let her affect him at all.

Could have. Should have. *Didn't.*

No—he'd kissed her. How freaking inspired! He'd put his dirty mitts all over her, because that was the kind of idiot he was.

All he'd wanted to do last night was undo the pain he'd seen on her face when he'd backed away from her. It was one hundred per cent pure instinct. Did she seriously not know that a beautiful, wet, virtually naked woman with fire in her eyes striding through the water towards him was the best part of fantasy? And it had scared the stuffing out of him, in that moment, because it had been happening. Because of how much he'd *wanted it* to happen.

And then Sera had seen his hesitation. And he might as well have struck her.

Kissing her was scarcely a better plan, but what kind of a man would he be if he'd let her leave that pool thinking she had somehow repulsed him.

The kind of man that did it just moments later, anyway, a tiny voice scolded.

No. He'd been in that kiss, too. He knew how it felt. How the two of them had combusted despite all the water. He'd stopped it before it had become something much harder to come back from. And he'd stopped it before he'd really done something that his bosses would haul him over the coals for. He'd done what he did best.

Retreat. To the place where things were clear-cut and simple and defined.

No one said you couldn't *want*, just that you couldn't *touch*. His mistake had been in thinking it was kinder to let Sera know how much he wanted.

What had happened after that wasn't kind at all.

Matteo's little face flashed across the morning sky. Mouth agape in silent grief, his damp little fingers pressed to the back window of the UN vehicle as the extraction team raced him away from the embassy in Cairo. Saving his life.

He'd learned nothing from that day.

'If you want to collect any messages or emails,' one of the other guides called out to the guests roaming around on top of the dune, 'this is your last chance. We get full-signal 4G up here. We'll be heading off in a few minutes.'

Brad glanced at his smartphone and saw that he had vastly more signal here than anywhere else in the resort. Made sense since they were closer to the comms satellites here than anywhere else in the desert.

Far, far below, Sera still hunkered down at the base of that one solitary tree, her knees pulled to her chest. As alone and stoic as the tree was. They still had a couple of weeks to go out here, together. In each other's pockets. And no matter how hardened Sera thought she was, she was going to suffer for all of it. Death by a thousand cuts. Unless he did what he was paid to do…

Protect her.

Brad brought his phone up to eye level, framed it with his keypad on the right and her distant, huddled form on its left and did the most decent thing he could.

He hit two on his speed dial.

For a big man with a heap of presence, Brad was pretty proficient at turning invisible. He tailed her everywhere his job description said he had to, but otherwise he kept a low profile all day after the duning and just let her be. He lurked in the shadows at breakfast and lunch, he left her to her thoughts in her suite, he kept a more than respectful distance when she went for walk.

Of course, proficiency was kind of his reason for being in this world, right? It was what floated his boat.

And what sank hers.

As 'it's-not-you-it's-me' speeches went, his had been pretty spectacular.

...one hundred per cent my loss...

Kissing her might not have been the most conventional let-you-down-easy technique but it had at least served to befuddle her mind enough that she didn't put up much of a fight. So in that regard it was fairly effective.

'Sera...'

He sank down in the chair across from her in the restaurant, grave focus on his handsome face, and the succulent bite she'd just forked into her mouth turned to ash. Something about his expression made her want to sit down. Except she already was.

'I wanted you to hear it from me first...'

Her breath immediately tightened. 'Is it Dad?' she croaked.

The clutch of fear and the flash of childhood memories between the thumps of her heart reminded her of how much she had to lose, even if Blaise hadn't always been the father of the year. He had his own protection detail, too, but they couldn't be everywhere, right?

'No, no,' Brad was quick to reassure and managed to look pained all over again. 'He's fine. Sorry.'

But he couldn't hold her gaze and he resorted to a kind of half-hearted scan of the perfectly secure restaurant to poorly disguise it.

Ice-cold crystals of certainty began to form in her chest cavity. Here it came…

'I've been reassigned,' he said simply. 'It's effective immediately.'

The crystals crackled with every challenging breath in and out. Did he seriously believe his lie wasn't totally transparent? That she would fail to grasp the incredible coincidence in timing? No, he'd *asked* to be transferred. To get away from the pressure she'd stupidly put on him.

Her gut balled up around the dinner she'd barely started, but he was giving her a vaguely gracious out and she wasn't going to pass up the chance to save some shred of dignity.

If it wasn't too late.

'You're in demand,' she squeezed out and hoped it came across lighter than it felt.

'It's a good opportunity,' he murmured. 'Some US corporates heading out to the Sheikh's oilfields.'

'That's a step up from babysitting.'

His big shoulders sagged. 'Sera—'

'No! It's good. It's the kind of work you prefer. Congratulations.' Consonants and vowels had never cost her so much. Nor sounded so hollow.

'My replacement arrived an hour ago. He's settling into my suite. I'll do a full handover with him tonight and head out first thing.'

'Hope he likes sharing a bed.' She couldn't quite muster up a chuckle. Her lungs wouldn't expand enough for it.

'I'll take the deck lounger one last time.'

Last time… Inner Sera whimpered. Her breath grew uneven. 'Your deck or mine?'

Grey, steady eyes bled regret. 'I wouldn't mind getting one last look at our oryx.'

Our oryx. Just how pathetic was it that she would wake early every day from now to see it, too, simply because they had it in common? And it would remind her of Brad. Until she left anyway, then what would she have?

The awful reality of what he'd just told her started to sink in. If only she'd kept her temper last night, if only she hadn't let the pain leak out all over him. If only she hadn't thrown herself at him then Brad might not be leaving now. She'd made it virtually impossible for him to stay, really, by compromising the professional integrity he valued so highly.

How could she be angry with someone for acting in accordance with their principles? Principles were what she respected most about him. His ethic and passion.

Just not when it meant he had to leave tomorrow.

It was only when her time had prematurely run out that she realised what two more weeks would have meant to her. And what the past couple weeks had. How a simple fortnight could feel like half a lifetime…when it was over. And it was only when she realised *that*, that it occurred to her what Brad had come to mean to her.

He would return to his apartment in Kafr Falaj and his schmick new assignment, and she would return to London, to whatever lingered of the press storm she'd fled, and to her father. Half a world away. And she would never see Brad again. Her only avenue to him was through the Sheikh, and the head of security for a gazillionaire royal was hardly about to divulge the personal information of one of his personnel. No matter how nicely you asked.

But asking Brad to stay in touch was not an option.

She at least had that much pride.

The futility and powerlessness of that began to

gnaw. She wanted to panic but she wanted to stay dignified, too. The reality was that two weeks was *not* a half a lifetime…it was just two weeks; and they would have faced this moment soon enough anyway. At New Year when she was due to leave. Just because a man kissed you half to death didn't mean he wanted to kiss you until he was old and grey.

They were never going to get happy ever after. Brad had just brought it forward a little.

'I'll be sorry to have to break another you in,' she said.

Don't go…

He flashed her that twisted smile that was his speciality. 'Think of the fun you'll have messing with the new guy's head.'

'Salim will be sorry not to get to show off his horses.'

Please, don't go…

'He'll live.'

She straightened her cutlery either side of her plate until it was perfect, then murmured to the tablecloth, 'Thank you for taking such good care of me.'

Don't leave me…

'It was my pleasure, Sera.'

Not what she'd meant. Somehow in the past two weeks Brad had done more for her aching heart than anyone in the years before it, without even trying. Despite the dismal ending. Kind of patched it over. Made it slightly better.

Or maybe that was just hope. Wasn't that what she'd started to let herself feel? Believe?

That maybe this time things were going to work out.

But then a tanned hand slid into view and over her own. It drew her gaze upwards.

'Sera,' he started, a deep, pained shadow behind his eyes. Of course he was feeling it, he wasn't an unkind man. She couldn't love an unkind man.

Oh, God...

'You're going to be fine,' he assured her through the ringing of realisation in her ears. 'Dwayne is a good operator.'

But she couldn't find the words to reply. Everything inside her was too busy spinning at the enormity of what she'd just realised.

I think I might love you.

He pushed back from the table at her silence. 'Okay, I'll leave you to your dinner. When you wake up tomorrow, Dwayne will be on duty and I'll be gone.'

Her pulse kicked into a panic at the very thought of him disappearing into the desert, or the city or some oilfield. Of being entire oceans away from her. Anonymous and untraceable. But life had prepared her well for this moment; she'd cared for people before and watched them move on, so she'd had plenty of practice. But it still wasn't easy to not say what her head and heart were screaming.

I love you.

'Okay.'

And then—on that pathetic parting croak—it was done.

Brad was up and back standing in the shadows doing his job and she was left to hold it together while he watched. Excruciating! The harder she tried to master her breathing, the choppier it became until the intolerable fear that she'd break down in tears in front of him and everyone else in the restaurant prompted her to fold her serviette onto the table and stand up. She waved away the concerned staff, assuring them the meal was faultless as always, and hurried past them for the nearest exit. Hiding in the bathroom wouldn't do anything to quell the tornado of emotion churning through her—she needed to be free…moving…

not trapped in a small space with Brad waiting outside the door.

Witness to it all.

He practically had to jog to keep up with her furious pace back along the pathway, and she couldn't hear his soft footfalls, but she didn't turn around, didn't try to speak to him. She knew he was there. Exactly when had she become able to *sense* his presence? She fumbled the key at the door to her suite but slipped in and closed it hard behind her before Brad could step forward from the shadows to clear the room. Then she killed the suite's nightlights, climbed into bed fully clothed and pulled the covers up to her chin in the pitch darkness.

As fortified as she could get in this wide-open place.

CHAPTER ELEVEN

BRAD STORMED AROUND the luxury suite at midnight, shoving his belongings into his bag as he found them. The beauty of travelling light—it only took minutes to pack again. Lucky he'd done what he had to do by phone earlier that morning, because sitting in that restaurant looking at the watery courage in Sera's eyes as she desperately tried to hang on to some dignity, he wasn't sure he would have been able to follow it through.

But he needed to be gone from this assignment.

Sera was too precious and too fragile a creature to withstand him stomping around finding his way with her. He was a soldier. Destroying stuff was his speciality. She needed someone more rock-solid to watch over her. Someone with more discipline.

Someone with some personal fortitude.

She'd been let down by every man she'd ever known. What made him think he'd be any different?

He'd already proved he couldn't be trusted with fragile hearts.

Lucky for him Sera had more strength than she suspected, because if even one of those tears she'd been holding back in the restaurant had tumbled down her cheek he would have been a goner.

He paused in the middle of the suite, staring blindly at the items he'd shoved in his duffel, his eyes locked on one in particular. A rolled-up watercolour he'd found tucked away in the back of the resort's little shop of Arabian curiosities. Some artist who had painted Omar while staying at Al Saqr. A beautiful work that somehow captured the bird's vulnerability as well as his essential strength.

It had reminded him immediately of Sera.

He'd bought it for her in one of his undisciplined moments. Because he'd wanted to give her one positive Christmas memory, at least, to hold to her heart.

But instead of saving Christmas, he'd just added to her litany of sucky associations. Future Sera wasn't going to remember the beautiful deserts of Umm Khoreem or Omar or the gorgeous light that she'd discovered this December. She was going to remember the fool who'd rejected her already bruised heart. Who'd kissed her then coldly turned his back.

He hadn't saved Christmas for her at all. He'd pretty much nailed its coffin lid shut.

Outstanding work, Kruger.

And this was why he couldn't have nice things.

Behind him, a strong fist sounded on his door just once, and he crossed to open up to Dwayne Cooper, Sera's new protection. Dwayne was exactly what Sera needed. A pro. A good and loyal operator. He'd been doing this most of his life and he'd never done anything more than his job.

Dwayne wasn't going to make Sera feel any better, but he sure as hell wouldn't make her feel any worse.

It was hours before Sera heard him again, but she was still dry-eyed and awake after Brad finished his handover with the new guy and her ears immediately heard the soft fall of his boots as he stepped up from the desert sands onto her deck. The deck lounger creaked a little as he sank down into it for what was left of the night and then all was silent again outside.

By the time the curtains started to glow with the telltale arrival of dawn, her arms were cramping and her fingers had fully seized up. She imagined their oryx—all aslosh with pool water—pootling back down the dune front to join its fellows for the day, and Brad sitting up murmuring his final farewells to it.

It was hard not to whisper a few of her own.

The deck lounger squeaked, boots gently touched down on the deck and then—just moments later— there was a soft knock at the glass door. Barely more than the scratching of some kind of wild creature. She remained frozen in her feather fortress until the scratching ceased. Then the footsteps tracked around the suite, stepped off the deck and were gone. In the heightened silence, she heard two deep voices speaking low somewhere nearby and an eternity later a pair of heavier boot falls on her deck. A heavier creak on *Brad's* deckchair. And the slurp of coffee.

He was *a slurper*, this new guy.

Inexplicably, that was what ended her emotional siege. Brad had never slurped. He just sipped. He tasted and appreciated his coffee. He valued it. He knew what mattered in life.

Unlike Sir Slurps-a-Lot out there.

'Hey!' she said, flinging the door open to a surprised stranger.

Dwayne practically tipped his coffee all over his immaculate suit in his haste to get to his feet. 'Morning, Ms Blaise—'

She ignored his greeting.

'How much trouble is he going to be in with the Sheikh for not finishing this job?' she demanded.

To his credit, the guy didn't even pause. Or pretend to misunderstand. 'None.'

Really? 'He made it seem like such a big deal.'

'He quit, so it doesn't matter what they think.'

'What?'

'He and the boss mutually agreed to wind up his contract.'

No. That wasn't right. Work was everything to Brad. Work and reputation. He couldn't just chuck it in. Not over her. She was not going to be responsible for another good man losing his job.

'What time is his pickup?' she cried, dashing back inside.

'N-now,' he stammered. 'He's going home right now.'

Home. To Australia? Somehow that felt even farther away.

'I need my guide!' she called out, hauling on a pair of jeans over her little pyjama shorts and not caring that a stranger watched. 'And his SUV. Now!'

It took Dwayne just a moment or two to discover that Eric wasn't on until six a.m. and he reported that as he hung up her phone. 'They're sending someone else to get you.'

'No time to wait for a buggy pickup. I'll meet them at the vehicle.' She hopped out of the door, tugging a second trainer on, and set off in the direction of the resort's reception.

'Someone' turned out to be Aqil, who sat perched in one of Al Saqr's SUVs like an adolescent boosting a car that was way too powerful for him.

He looked totally ready for adventure.

'Can you drive this thing?' Sera called, leaping in beside him. Dwayne climbed straight in at the back, though he didn't look entirely pleased to be there. He was probably used to taking shotgun.

'More or less.'

Good enough. 'Floor it.'

He did, but the distant dust plume that was Brad's ride was very distant and they didn't seem to be making any headway in catching it. And if he reached the highway then she would lose him because she could hardly run through the International Airport in a low-cut pyjama top. Barely in England. Absolutely not here.

Not unless she fancied a second round with the authorities.

'Can we go off road?'

'Not if you want to catch them.' Regret-filled brown eyes glanced at her, as though she was the first person he'd ever failed. 'I'm sorry.'

Once again Al Saqr's immaculate training meant their staff needed no explanation and Aqil caught on pretty quick. He fumbled with one hand in his pocket and tossed Sera his mobile phone. 'Please press four.'

The polite request was so ridiculously at odds with a woman still in her pyjama top and a bear of a man in a dark suit forcing him to drive like a getaway driver, she found it impossible not to laugh. She set the phone to speaker and pressed the keypad. Someone answered in the local tongue. Aqil fired off a reply that was equally unfathomable. A question back and again and a spray of incomprehensible but lyrical Arabic, then he signed off and nodded at her to disconnect the call.

'The security guard will hold them.'

Of course! She'd totally forgotten Al Saqr's high-security entrance. 'Oh, I could kiss you, Aqil.'

His delighted dimples flashed but he didn't slow down. He was Guest Liaison and not a guide—he probably didn't get all that many chances to drive the company vehicles like a rally pro. They bumped and bounced over the compacted sand, then onto the limestone, and finally onto the asphalt. Just moments later, the boom gate and massive fences came into view. A black SUV sat there patiently idling in front of the lowered boom, the driver and security guard leaning on the boom gate, having a casual conversation while they waited.

As Aqil applied the brakes Brad got out of the back of the SUV, a deep frown scoring his face, and turned towards them. He braced his whole weight on two slightly spread feet, ready for anything. It was only at the last minute that Aqil slowed and then pulled to a gentle stop as though they'd been out for nothing more than a Sunday drive.

'What the hell, Sera?'

His words were for her but his dark frown was for Dwayne, who followed her out of the bigger vehicle.

'I didn't get to say goodbye,' she said simply, suddenly stunningly self-conscious about the four pairs of male eyes witnessing this scene. And her pyjama top.

'I knocked.'

'I know. I ignored you.'

He shook his head. 'So you thought an early morning heart-starter was in order?'

Her colour was high. She could feel it in her own cheeks.

'Stay,' she blurted. And it stunned him into silence. 'I'll hire you privately, to stay…here.'

With me, she couldn't quite bring herself to say.

'Al Saqr's a little out of my budget,' he hedged and the fact he did nearly robbed her of the courage she needed to spread her ribs wider.

'You can stay in my suite,' she breathed. 'On the deck or…not.'

God. She was just terrible at this. But didn't she have to take a risk at some point? Or was she going to let fear keep her cowed forever? Brad was not Mark. The way she felt when she was with him was like nothing she'd ever known before.

Tiny forks appeared at the corner of both eyes. 'I can't, Sera.'

Was he going to cite the local law at her as she had once with him? Because she was more than ready to commit another crime if it meant she got a second chance with Brad. And there was always a first time for him…

She kicked up her chin. 'I'm not worth breaking a few rules for?'

'I'm not…I can't…' Breath hissed out of him. 'I don't want to hurt you any more than I already have, Sera.'

Just when she'd felt sure her new-found courage would be rewarded. Did the universe not realise how difficult it was for her to open herself up like this? But having started, she couldn't stop. Too much rode on it.

'Then what's stopping you? Because it's sure as hell not your job. Dwayne told me you've quit the Sheikh's team.'

Angry eyes swung towards Dwayne, who very carefully kept his focus on the horizon. Like a trained pro. But when Brad's came back to hers, they weren't harsh. Quite the opposite.

'I think I'm stopping me, Sera,' he murmured.

It was the pain that got her attention; it shadowed his gaze and thickened his voice. His leaving would hurt her, but staying was hurting him. Somehow. And she didn't want to hurt him. But she had to understand. And she would never forgive herself if she didn't try just one last time.

'Some things are more important than rules, Brad. Aren't they?'

His eyes were filled with sorrow. 'Some things are, yes.'

Oh.

Awful, horrible awareness came into focus the way the desert sharpened around her as the sun rose each morning.

Some things were more important than rules. But she wasn't one of those things.

The fact she was so unprepared for that answer was almost a greater surprise than hearing him say it. Had she really learned nothing from her past? The whole work cover was just to save him from having to hurt her feelings by rejecting her outright.

He'd lied to protect her.

Of course he had. That was his job.

'I'm not a good fit for you, Sera. I'm not…' Words seemed to elude him. 'I can't be responsible for your emotional well-being.'

Everything in her froze.

Was she that much of a basket case? That he didn't want to be anywhere near her? Was she just too high maintenance?

'Okay…' Her voice was deeper than she wanted. 'Sera—'

'No!' Her arms curled around her torso to rub her bare arms. God…she'd chased him. In her pyjamas. With witnesses. 'You should go, then. I get it. I'm sorry that I pressured you to stay. That was unfair of me.'

He shrugged out of his coat, transferred his wallet into his trousers pocket and draped the coat around her shoulders to give her some warmth. And some very overdue modesty.

'There's no pressure, Sera. Don't let this set you back—'

No. She could not stand here and listen to a man who was rejecting her lecture her about how to handle rejection.

She could only bend so much before she'd break.

So she just nodded. And backed away.

'We had a safe word,' she joked, miserably, trying to make the pain go away. 'You should have just used it.'

His deep eyes softened almost unbearably and his big hand came up to brush her cheek as he killed her soul.

'Capsicum,' he murmured.

It meant *goodbye*. It meant *I'm sorry*. And it meant *it's over*.

It took everything she had not to let the sob that broke within her actually come out. But her body jerked as it imploded painfully and silently inside. She didn't call out a farewell as Brad ducked his head back into the SUV. She didn't wave as the boom lifted and he set off again, airport bound. She didn't cry as all three of them bumped, slow and silent, back up Al Saqr's endless driveway because she was too emotionally hollow to feel much of anything. She just tucked Brad's coat more closely around her and buried her nose into it, letting the slight hint of his scent comfort her.

Yay. That had to be a new personal low.

CHAPTER TWELVE

HAD SOMETHING HAPPENED to the light out here? Maybe the seasons were changing as Christmas Day loomed? Eric had answered politely in the negative, and assured her that last week's light was much the same as this week's.

Except that nothing else about the past seven days was the same as the weeks before it.

Dwayne had settled easily into the role of desert protector, and she had managed to settle obediently into the role of protect*ed*. Compliant and co-operative. Dwayne must have wondered if he was monitoring the wrong woman; she was nothing like the one that Brad had probably warned him about in his handover. The two of them spoke, but nothing interesting. He smiled and laughed on cue but it was always respectfully hollow and Sera never really felt like joining him. Or teasing him. Or challenging him. Or watching him swim, shirtless. Until she wondered how much of her day-to-day interaction with Brad had actually been foreplay in disguise.

Had his leaving even sucked the golden out of this beautiful place? She flicked through the images on her laptop and tried to compare them dispassionately. On screen, the sunrises were just as blazing, the mountains loomed equally powerfully and the light was still rich and gorgeous. She flipped the lid shut on a hiss and stared out.

So it was just her, then.

'Time to go,' Dwayne said, knocking firmly as he nudged open her front door.

That was his style. He never came in except to clear the room. He never camped out on her deck. He never engaged as she undertook the daily desert experiences. Which was fine because she didn't want that from him.

But, Lord, how she missed it. The desert now felt as isolated and empty as Brad had warned her it could be.

'What are we doing, again?' she asked Dwayne distractedly as she rose and moved towards the door. He'd reminded her the night before but whatever he'd said was gone now.

'Archery.'

Good, she was just in the mood to shoot something. Lots of somethings. Fortunately for her and her terrible aim, the archery field had nothing but a big, empty sand dune behind it, so when she missed—and she surely would—her arrows wouldn't go whizzing towards anything with a pulse. Her mood wasn't so dark she wanted to start killing the wildlife she'd come to adore.

In her mind, Brad chuckled at her joke.

Sigh. There he was again.

It really didn't take much; the vaguest connection and some Brad-related memory managed to sneak through her shields the same way sand got into everything here. Never mind that she had a lifetime of memories before Brad, it seemed that her recall was firmly fixed to the two weeks she'd known him.

It was crazy. And a little bit sad. And she hoped it would stop soon.

Was this what a break-up felt like? You had to be in a relationship to break up from it, didn't you? And you had to be open to people for relationships to form. What would have happened if she'd been braver? If she'd let herself be open to the affections of others despite the risk of losing it? Maybe she'd have had more joy in her young life. Maybe she'd be married with a dozen kids by now. And maybe she wouldn't be as high maintenance as she apparently was.

Or maybe she'd just have had more loss.

There was one very obvious upside to being closed down, emotionally…

Dwayne gave her his arm, needlessly, to help her into the low buggy that came for them but she took it anyway because she just didn't have the energy to protest. The archery range was lovely, tucked in on both sides by Sidr trees filled with the pendulous, scrappy nests of tiny birds and backlit by the morning sunrise. Dwayne retreated to a guest bench in the distance and left her with Eric, who took her through her archery basics.

She glanced at him briefly.

Eric was a good-looking guy. Maybe she could be open to Eric and maybe he'd fill that empty place inside her just as Brad had? Although Eric's job depended on his professional relationships with his guests.

Pfff… Story of her life.

She really needed to start meeting some men who weren't paid *not* to get involved with her.

'Robin Hood is total rubbish,' Eric said to her quietly while demonstrating the traditional Arabian archery technique, working hard to draw her attention. 'Carrying a quiver of arrows on your back would have been impractical and slow as you bounced around on horse or on foot. Arabian archers wore arrows at their hip and armed with three or four at a time for rapid firing.'

She should have been spellbound. It *was* fascinating. But all Sera wanted to do was get to the good part. The part that would make her feel better.

'Can I just shoot something, Eric?' she said. 'I'll come back another day for the history.'

He looked at her, long and hard, but took no offence. In fact, whatever he saw in her face put a gentle kind of understanding on his. He was out here alone at Christmas, too, after all. So, they jumped straight to the firing part. It took her no time to learn enough to get it roughly right and— just as she'd imagined—the cold, slow precision with which she loaded, drew and fired at the distant target rings suited her mood perfectly. Every distant *thwack* brought her a sore kind of satisfaction deep in her chest.

Like pushing your tongue on a toothache until you winced.

'Wow,' Eric said, staring at the cluster of arrows

peppering the distant target. 'Remind me never to cross you.'

When she ran out of her own arrows—and then Eric's—Sera moved into the shade as he jogged down and collected them all back up for a rerun. Only a few of them were buried to the fins in the sand dune behind the target. That was vaguely satisfying.

'Listen,' he said as the biting sun forced them to pack up. 'You've done every activity we offer...'

He wasn't kidding—ballooning, dune drives, nature walks, falconry, spa experiences, souk visits, camel rides, astronomy, even the half-day caving special. A busy mind was a sane mind, right?

She laughed but it was empty.

'Except one,' he continued.

She turned her face up to his. 'Really? What did I miss?'

'The desert dinner.'

Instant ache returned to her gut, undoing all her positive archery therapy. 'That's a couples' thing.'

'You don't *have* to be a couple to participate.'

'I'm not going to make your staff lug all that gear out into the desert and cook for one.'

'Look, Sera, it's romantic, yes. But the desert is beautiful at night and it's Christmas Eve tonight.

That's why I thought of you. You can't sit alone in your suite on Christmas Eve.'

Uh…yeah, she could. She'd seen in a lot of Christmases that way.

But the thought of doing another one like that suddenly did seem unbearable. She could fake it the rest of the year, but Christmas really put a spotlight on how alone she was. Made it very hard to ignore. Or deny. At least this way she could have a unique experience. Something to fondly look back on for future Christmases. If she ever found the courage to think of these weeks again.

'Can they do it without the towering torches?' she hedged. Giant candles would do nothing to reduce the glaring *non*-romance of the occasion.

'Not if you want to see. And keep the vipers away.'

'What about ditching the cosy camp table for two, then?' Nothing said *alone* quite like an empty place setting opposite.

'We can do that. A couple of cushions on the rugs instead. And a telescope. We wouldn't normally include it but you're such a long-stay guest, management have okayed pretty much anything where you're concerned.'

She gnawed her lip.

'In my experience,' he murmured, 'nothing heals as fast as perspective. How tiny and short our lives are compared to the great carousel of worlds around us.' He casually hiked the archery gear up under his arm. 'Anyway, think about it and let me know by noon.'

He turned and was halfway to where Dwayne now stood waiting when she called out.

'I don't have to think about it, Eric. It sounds amazing. Count me in.'

She couldn't mope forever.

Al Saqr's staff simply weren't going to let her.

Eric's smile was almost relief. Maybe a sad guest was an untenable challenge to him.

Dwayne shadowed her back to the resort's hub for breakfast and, on the way, they saw the morning camel trek returning in the distance. She'd seen Salim just once since Brad left and he'd nodded politely but not managed eye contact. As if she held no real interest now that she had no connection to Brad.

Ugh, everywhere she went…

Breakfast was stunning as always and she forced herself to dig into the plate of scrambled eggs liberally dosed with goat's cheese and red pepper. Her fork stuttered as she realised…

Capsicum.

And suddenly Brad was intruding again.

Okay, she thought, slamming her cutlery down, *this has to stop.*

Not only was it infuriating to have no control whatsoever over her own mind but she really wanted to go back to enjoying her food.

She spent the rest of the day lounging around her suite, reading, thinking, enormous parts of it just staring at the sand and losing time. She purposefully had an early lunch since her evening meal was timed to coincide with sunset, and as the sun drew closer to the horizon Dwayne tapped on her door to rouse her for the desert dinner experience.

For one.

Eric ferried her out towards the sinking sun to a place in the sands where a number of rugs were laid out, piled high with cushions. Four torches already burned at north, south, east and west of the little camp and covered dishes sat, waiting, on a beautifully carved plinth gently surrounded by perfect glass baubles. The kind you'd normally hang on a tree. It was such a gentle and culturally appropriate nod to Christmas it was hard not to appreciate it. She reached her fingers out and brushed them along one smooth, glassy edge remembering the designer ones that had hung on her father's enormous tree back home.

Somewhere deep inside she'd hoped that travelling to somewhere they didn't do Christmas would protect her from the loneliness she associated with it. But who was she kidding? The loneliness just travelled with her. It was all she'd ever known.

And that wasn't going to change all on its own.

There were more baubles in the ornate cooler box set off to one side. Pretty carved ones this time, buried in amongst the water, wine, and the juice she'd gone so crazy for since arriving. And there was a bottle of champagne nestled in there, too.

Yeah...that wasn't going to get any love tonight.

She glanced back over to the SUV parked at a discreet distance and saw Eric and Dwayne within, each holding something that could have been water or it could have been beer. She was hardly going to begrudge them the latter on Christmas Eve. Or make Dwayne stand out on the sand, parched, while she enjoyed a lovely dinner. She poured herself a juice and wandered over to the low-range telescope Eric had set up.

The stars could be her company tonight!

She peered off into the desert's far distance with

the telescope while the sky was still light, slowly working her way back in, stopping now and again for small curiosities. She saw a group of Al Saqr's guests on a guided sunset nature walk and Salim on some kind of private exercise with just two of his camels and one guest plodding through the sand beside him.

And oryx, of course, everywhere. Migrating to their nocturnal foraging grounds.

As soon as the beautiful sunset concluded, she doused the two largest of her torches—and kidded herself it was to improve her view of the heavens and not lessen the romance—then returned to her rugs and just sat, listening to the vast nothing, a woven wrap around her to keep her warm. Breathing in the natural, sweet air. Smelling the fragrant oils that burned in the remaining torches. It was all very…Arabian. She knelt in front of the plinth and uncovered all the dishes, then filled her plate with the tasty treats. Some she already knew, some were new. The sorts of offerings the three Kings of the Orient might have eaten as they tracked a bright star. Christmassy yet…not. It reminded her of the celebration at Salim's camp and she half wished for the apple-flavoured shisha and Salim's son on his twangy instrument in the background.

But eating alone never took very long, so Sera stretched the evening out by lying on the rugs between snacks and staring up at the endless starry blackness above.

Thinking.

So many stars. The closest were suns in solar systems much like our own. Some were the combined light of distant galaxies full of suns. Yet others were the combined light of galaxy-filled universes so far away it was nearly incomprehensible. She reached out a fist beside her and curled it full of sand, then let the sands escape through her fingers, luxuriating in the soft sensation as it filtered through the gaps in her grasp. There had to be as many worlds out there as grains of sand in this desert. Billions upon billions. How many of them had life that we would recognise? How many of them were home to bipedal apes who'd built civilisations and achieved space flight and conquered the diseases that constrained their population? How many of them had deserts, and teeny, tiny people having a lonely Christmas Eve dinner right now under the gaze of a trillion other worlds?

How many of them hurt as much as she did?

The heavens turned right through the delicious fruity pudding she eventually remembered to serve herself—another nod to the season. And still she lay there in the torchlight, the solid comfort of the earth at her back and the mind-bending vastness of space in front of her. With nothing but her own breath in her ears.

Except that wasn't entirely true; from beyond the visible circle cast by her torches, she could hear a kind of chuffing that she recognised from the oryx that visited her pool each morning. She slowly pushed upright. Wild oryx were less wild within the reserve's fences but they still had very sharp horns that she didn't want to get on the pointy end of.

Then, the chuffing became a grunt and she heard the distinctive plod of enormous feet on sand.

Camels.

Did they have free-ranging camels within Al Saqr's lands? She glanced over to where the SUV sat in the same darkness that surrounded her and she threw Dwayne and Eric an urgent look, trusting that they would notice.

And then the camels came...two of them, right on the edge of the torch's circle of light. All legs at first but then someone gave a whistle and the one in front kneeled awkwardly, protesting, followed closely by the one behind.

'Salim?'

She knew him by his manner with the camels and by his height on the edge of the shadows. Lovely to see him but…why? No one had told her a night camel ride was part of the desert-dinner experience? She wasn't really dressed for it.

Salim nodded but came no closer. Instead, he turned and glanced behind him anxiously as if waiting for something to happen.

Suddenly, every warning Brad had ever given her about bad guys on camels came rushing back. Where were Dwayne and Eric? Anything could have happened to them out there in the darkness and she wouldn't know. But surely if someone was going to make a grab for a celebrity's daughter they'd do it by vehicle, even here in the desert? Still, she bent her knees on instinct and readied herself for a dark, desert dash. However short-lived it might be.

God, she wished she'd paid more attention to the direction they'd come out here in.

'It's okay, Sera. You're safe.'

Lucky her legs were already bent. It saved them from buckling as Brad's voice carried to her in the half-darkness. His tall, strong silhouette followed it into the circle of light as he strode towards her out of the darkness like some kind of mirage.

Or desert delusion.

Everything in her squeezed up hard. 'Brad?'

Probably not as welcoming as he might have hoped. But that was what you got for scaring the stuffing out of someone.

'Were you expecting some other camel-mounted stranger in the dark?'

'I wasn't expecting anyone.'

'Sorry for the subterfuge,' he murmured, stepping up to the edge of the area designated by the torches.

It physically hurt to look at his face again.

'I didn't know if you'd come, otherwise.'

Even now, her instinct to protect herself was strong. All she wanted to do was fling herself at him, but she forced her feet to stay rooted in the sands within the torched area. As though light could keep her safe.

'What are you doing here? I thought you were in Australia.'

He maintained a careful distance from her. 'No. I never left Umm Khoreem.'

'But...you were headed home.' Except then it

occurred to her that he'd never actually said the words *air* or *port*. 'Weren't you?'

'I've been staying out at the camp, with my uncle,' he replied with a grateful glance back at Salim, who had busied himself talking low to his beloved camels.

Questions spun around her addled mind like the wild fringes of a tornado but finally settled on the simplest one. 'Why?'

'He's been helping me.'

'No. I mean, why did you stay?'

His hands rose up either side of him and he looked as if he was struggling to find the easiest explanation, too. 'I couldn't leave.'

Old caution kept her from reading too much into that. For all she knew his passport might have expired.

He hovered, awkwardly, on the edge of the circle of light. 'Can I come in?'

Rushing forward and dragging him in was inappropriate, right?

'Sure. Wipe your feet.'

God, how she'd missed that low chuckle! Behind her, the SUV rumbled to expensive life as soon as she made the single gesture of welcome and began to reverse down the dune. She turned and stared at the slash of its headlights as Eric switched them back on.

'Neither of them were going to leave unless you were okay about me being here.'

She watched them rumble away. 'Too bad, now, if I'm not.'

'If you are not, Sera,' Salim pledged from the edge of darkness, 'then I will escort you home on his camel and Bradley can stumble back in the dark with the scorpions.'

That little show of solidarity made her Salim's for life.

'Is that why you were awkward earlier this week?' she called to the shadows. 'Because you were harbouring a fugitive?'

Salim chuckled. Or it could have been a camel... Impossible to distinguish.

Brad took another step. 'Will you sit?'

'Um, no.' This was a conversation best had standing.

'Okay.' Uncertainty stained his voice. And she'd never heard him be anything other than totally confident.

'Here,' he began, reaching back over his shoulder and gently pulling out a scroll of paper bound with a bright bow. 'I got this for you.'

Of all the things she'd imagined about this evening, camels, Brad and gifts were never one of them.

'It's a Christmas gift,' he clarified as she stood motionless.

'Christmas is tomorrow.'

'I know but... Just in case. You can keep it sealed until tomorrow if you want.'

Pfff... Did he not know her at all? She tugged on the loose end of the bow and the pretty ribbon fell away, allowing the scroll to unspool in her hands. Then she stepped closer to one of the torches and held it up. It was a watercolour, in the deep browns and golds of the desert, filled with a very familiar face.

Her breath backed up behind the sudden fist in her throat. 'Omar.'

'I thought he'd be a good memory of your trip. Something to hold on to when you're...'

Gone.

She wanted to clutch the image to her chest and never let go, but she didn't want to mark the perfect parchment. It took all her discipline to roll it back up and retie the ribbon. But then she clasped it close.

'Merry Christmas, Sera.'

'You came back to give me this?' she finally said.

'Only in part.'

No. She wasn't going to beg. Or guess. If he had something to say then let him say it. And then let him leave again.

'This past week has been good for me,' he began carefully.

Less so for me...

'Spending time with Salim,' he went on. 'Talking. He's helped me understand...a lot.'

'About?'

'Myself mostly. A few of the wrong turns I've taken.'

'Like what?'

'Most recently... Leaving the Sheikh's service the way I did.' His Adam's apple danced. 'Leaving you the way I did.'

So...what? He'd come back to break her heart more nicely?

'Weren't they the same thing?'

His eyes fell. 'They weren't, Sera. I left my job because I let them down.' He sucked in a deep breath. 'I left you because I was afraid.'

'Of what?' she pressed.

'Of failing.'

Her heart squeezed again, but this time it was for

him. For the blame she heard in his quiet words. 'Failing who?'

'People I was supposed to protect.' He took a breath. 'Matteo. You.'

There was just so much in that statement and she wasn't ready yet to face part of it.

'Matteo made it—'

'I nearly got him killed,' he urged. 'This innocent kid with so much life in him. I knew we were bonding and I let it flourish. I enjoyed it.' His eyes dropped. 'I never should have let myself grow close to him in the first place. I should have pushed him away.'

Sera took a long breath. 'By "him" you mean me, right? You think of me like Matteo?'

Like a seven-year-old child... Maybe she was. Had she really come far from the days when she would have done anything for her daddy's attention?

Dark lines—exaggerated by the sharp light from the low-burning torches—appeared between his brows. 'I thought it was going to be fine, that you were bolshie and tough as nails. I only had to worry about your physical safety. And keeping you off the internet,' he joked weakly.

'You said you didn't want to be responsible for my emotional well-being.'

Saying it out loud was scarcely more comforting than remembering the words on his lips.

'I said I *couldn't*, Sera. I didn't trust myself with anyone else's heart. If I thought for one second I'd be any good at all for you, emotionally, I would do whatever it took. Whatever you needed.'

The scarred organ in her chest began to hammer with an optimism she'd never imagined it could possibly have.

'I just needed you to stay,' she said simply.

He bundled her hands into his, begging her understanding. 'I *broke his heart*, Sera. A vulnerable little boy. I did more harm than good.'

'You might think that,' she said. 'But there's nothing good about letting a child think you don't care about them. Someone that they spend *every single* day with. Trust me on that.'

'But his suffering—'

'Would have been drawn out over months,' she urged. 'And it would have been personal. And it would have changed him forever. At least this way he had a conflict to blame for losing you and his parents to help him through it, rather than thinking it was *his* fault. That he was simply not good enough to love.'

The awful words echoed around the empty desert. Loud and sore.

Brad blinked in the flickering light. 'That's what you believed?'

'That's what I still believe.' She laughed. 'No matter how grown-up I try and be about it, it's still there in my foundations… Lurking. Because that's the message I got whenever someone kept me at a distance, whenever Dad chose his music over me, whenever some boy decided I wasn't worth the hassle. Whenever anyone used me for my connections.'

'Your father—'

'Shouldn't ever have *been* a father. I know that, logically. I suspect he does, too. He's way too absorbed in his own achievements and success. Don't get me wrong, I love him because he's my dad, but I drove myself into the ground trying to earn his respect and his love. I tried to substitute it with those around me but—wouldn't you know it?— they didn't love me either! That kind of reinforcement has a way of sticking in a kid's brain.'

She'd been staring into the low flames rather than risk seeing pity in Brad's gaze, but she looked back at him now. 'At least your Matteo had the love and respect of a man he worshipped. No matter how badly it ended. That is a *good* thing, Brad. Not something to mourn.'

Brad stared at her so long she thought maybe she was going to have to order him to blink. But, finally, he did. 'I never thought about it that way.'

'Obviously!' She snorted. 'You just leapt straight to the conclusion that you couldn't be trusted with someone's heart. The most trustworthy person I've ever known...'

Confusion washed over him. 'You're angry?'

'Yes, I'm angry. Because you've beaten yourself up unnecessarily for years over this and I'm guessing you haven't even sent that kid so much as a postcard since Cairo?'

'I didn't want to—'

'Right, so he's suffered unnecessarily for two years wondering what the hell he did wrong or whether you even survived the conflict.' She stepped up close and shoved him square in the chest, then couldn't quite bring herself to lower her hands. 'And I've suffered unnecessarily for a whole week wondering *what the hell* I have to do to be worthy of someone's love.'

'Sera—' His voice cracked.

Her fingers curled in the fabric of his shirt and she pulled herself up towards Brad's mouth. He caught her just as her lips met his. Every cell in her body celebrated. Like her, they'd thought they'd never ever taste him again. That gorgeous, rare, delicious flavour. He slid one strong arm around her to keep her fixed to him.

'Why are men such idiots?' she finally whispered against his mouth. 'We could have been doing that all week.'

'Because women mess with our minds until we don't know which way is up.'

'So this is my fault?' she challenged.

'No,' he murmured. 'I'm pretty sure you're the only sane one in this conversation. How did you get so smart?'

'Blood, sweat and tears.'

Oh, so many tears.

One of the camels snorted, and Sera remembered Brad's uncle sitting in the wings witnessing all these very *un*-politically correct displays of affection. She eased herself away from Brad a little. But he wouldn't let her go far.

'So…' She cleared her throat. 'You're back?'

Warm breath tickled her face. 'I'm back.'

She wanted to be brave. She wanted to be the confident woman that Brad would give an easy nine to on the normality scale. But old habits died hard and she had no idea what it meant that he was actually standing here. Like a mirage come to life.

'Why are you back?'

To explain himself? For a while? For good?

'I forgot to do something before I left,' he said.

Her heart recoiled into its safe little corner, preparing for the worst. But she couldn't find the mettle to speak.

'Pretty unprofessional of me, actually, to leave without fulfilling my obligation as your personal security.'

She blinked at him in pained confusion and—as she so often did—she hid behind humour. 'Something I should have signed?'

'I neglected to do my assessment report. For your file.'

Paperwork. Her head spun. *Okay...*

'Maybe I could submit it now?'

She pushed away and put a healthy pace-length of cold air between them. 'If you must.'

But he wouldn't let her go far and he held on to her fingers, keeping her close.

'Seraphina Blaise,' he recited. 'Twenty-four. Passionate and talented daughter to a father who doesn't deserve her...'

The fist in her chest shot back. Hard.

'Spent her young life developing shields to protect herself from those who should have been protecting her.' He tugged her back towards him, gently. 'Amazingly resilient and optimistic considering how often she has been let down in life, but has no concept of her true personal courage.'

She bit the inside of her cheek to keep from sobbing.

'Found her own beauty and joy in the world and then used her talent to help others. Even broke the law in defence of those who couldn't defend themselves. Was surrendered by one parent, neglected by another, used by her friends, and—more recently—betrayed by a man she trusted to protect her.'

She peered up at him. His eyes glittered with unshed emotion and behind that something else lurked. Something she barely recognised. Something she surely should not trust.

It was rich and deep and so full of the kind of promises she never, ever let herself believe.

'Yet, for all of it, she still has more love lurking

in her elegant little finger than any of them have in their entire bodies.'

He drew those fingers to his lips.

'Including that man she trusted to defend her?' she squeezed out past her tight throat.

'Especially that man,' Brad breathed. 'He's beginning to suspect he never had any idea what love was really about.'

'You didn't betray me,' she said, stepping up to him. 'You just left.'

'The biggest betrayal of all. I promise never to do it again.'

In any other two people, this was where the man would fall to his knees and declare undying love. In any other two people, the woman would throw herself into his arms and they'd live happily ever after. The End.

But they weren't any other two people.

He was proud, complicated Brad. She was cautious, baggage-laden Sera. The couple on any one of those distant planets circling above them might do things differently but—in this desert, on this planet—this man standing before her knew that she needed more than just to hear the words.

She needed to *believe* them.

And seeing was believing.

He took her hands in his, then raised them out to their sides, standing open and vulnerable before her. Exposed. Truth pouring from his warm gaze. Silently offering her everything that he was and wasn't.

Weakening himself so that she could be strong.

'Oh, my God,' she choked as she stared up into his unguarded eyes. 'Do you—?'

The lessons of her childhood weren't easy to forget. Every part of her screamed at her not to say it. Not to risk it. But he was going to stand there, silently, until she found the courage to use the words herself. She dug deep and found a little faith—in Brad, who would never intentionally set her up for hurt. In herself.

And that was certainly something new.

'Do you love me?' she whispered.

And somehow it came out not as a raw question, but as a truth. Wonderful and real.

Joy flooded into his eyes. 'Apparently that's a thing I do now.'

She, more than just about anyone, had every reason not to trust that look, but… She couldn't help the massive, teary smile. 'You love me.'

He matched it. 'You say that like it's a completely impossible miracle.'

'It is!'

'Why? You're amazing.'

'Because it just doesn't happen.' Not to her.

'It hasn't happened to me before now,' he admitted. 'That doesn't make it inconceivable.'

Suddenly, standing this close to him and not touching became untenable. She threw her arms around his neck and buried herself there again, breathing him in, holding him as tightly as his sure grip.

'I think I fell for you the moment you started flirting with me on the way from the airport,' he confessed.

She chuckled. 'What part of me giving you hell did you take as flirting?'

'You were testing me, constantly. I knew that. You've been testing people all your life to see how far you can push them. Waiting for someone to care enough to push back.'

She lifted her head and blinked.

'Did I *create* the distance I was so sensitive to?'

'Maybe.' He stroked a lock of hair from her face with a soft knuckle. 'Lucky I'm so obstinate, huh?'

She shook her head. 'I thought I knew who I was…'

Brad kissed one eyelid, and then the other and the gesture turned her heart to mush.

'We have a lifetime to get to know each other,' he murmured. 'Or ourselves. Whichever is the most interesting.'

A lifetime? 'What… What are you saying?'

'That wasn't a proposal,' he cautioned. 'No pressure.'

But then he looked around. 'Although there really couldn't be a more perfect place for one. Or a night. Maybe we can come back here next Christmas Eve and have this conversation again.'

Relief washed through her. And excitement. All she could hear was 'we'.

But she kept her cool.

'You think Al Saqr will have us back?'

'I think Al Saqr can arrange just about anything we want. They're our own personal Santa Claus.'

'Do you think they would give me the real Omar as a Christmas gift?'

His chuckle rumbled against her ear. 'Not a chance. You'll have to settle for the painting.'

She sighed her disappointment but snuggled in closer. 'What about you, then?'

'Yeah—' he rested his strong chin on top of her head '—that one is definitely negotiable.'

'How is it that I feel like I've known you my whole life?' she whispered.

'Pretty long couple of weeks, huh?'

'Wonder if they'll all be that long.'

'I hope so. That'll make up for all the time we didn't have each other.'

Not *know* each other. *Have* each other.

Tears stung her eyes horribly and a fist curled tight around her vocal cords. She peered up at him again. 'You know you're the first person I've ever actually *had*?'

'Have. Hold.' Brad's eyes darkened. 'Worse. Better.'

She gnawed her lip. 'There could be a bit of worse.'

A chuckle rattled his chest again. 'To love. To cherish.'

'Until vipers do us part.'

She stretched up on her toes in the sand and met him as soon as she could. His lips on hers were better than any of Al Saqr's delicious morsels. Tastier and sweeter and the sort of thing that would linger long after it was gone. They pressed and roamed and nibbled and discovered, and hers mirrored them happily.

If he kissed her forever it would be too short.

'I love you, Brad Kruger.'

'You'd better,' he murmured against her lips. 'Or loving you back is going to get really awkward.'

EPILOGUE

HAVE. HOLD. BETTER. WORSE.

It was twelve months to the day before he said those words again. In the right order this time.

True to Brad's pledge, he'd brought her back to Al Saqr and the desert dinner experience to officially propose under the wide open skies. Sera had only made him sweat a little before throwing herself into his arms and they'd had the world's shortest engagement, marrying the very next day.

Al Saqr had gifted them the honeymoon suite.

Salim had insisted on the full use of his desert camp for the ceremony and made sure that only the best-looking camels were invited.

Sera glanced around at the many faces assembled under the grand Bedouin canopies: Salim's ever more numerous family, Brad's father who—just like his son—stood sure and protective over the wife who hadn't been back in her ancestral lands for thirty years. Sera's eyes tracked left. Over in the corner, Aaliyah and Eric pretended to ignore each other—but something about their body language said that Salim might have to manage another cross-cultural entanglement very soon.

Even Matteo and his father had made the long journey out here courtesy of a devilish piece of secrecy on her part.

Behind them, the traditional music of the hired musicians took a turn for the stranger as her father and his band joined in with their acoustic guitars. Possibly the first aging, Goth rock stars to ever grace a Bedouin camp and already Blaise was talking about a new musical direction featuring traditional Arabian instruments. Trust him to find a way to make her special day all about him.

Taboos were trampled, rules were bent, cultures were melded and—somehow—it all worked out just fine.

'This could have gone so badly,' Sera said softly when finally they had a moment alone together.

He took full advantage, whisking her into the shadows for a kiss. 'Never.'

'Look around you. There's a dozen international incidents just begging to occur.'

He shrugged. 'Someone else's problem tonight.'

She offered a mock gasp. 'My goodness, how far you've come, Bradley.'

His arms wrapped more tightly around her. 'It seems you've ruined me, Seraphina.'

Sera rested her head on his shoulder. 'You know what? If this is ruin, then I'm not interested in redemption.'

'How long will you love me?' he murmured.

She glanced up at the blanket of stars above them. 'Until the brightest of those burns out.'

'Good answer.' He chuckled.

'You?'

'Until you ask me to stop.'

'Stop? Are you kidding? I've waited my whole life for you.'

Those grey eyes fringed by those dark lashes… Ugh, it just melted her heart. And given what her heart had been through, that was saying something. But she'd rather a vulnerable heart to a hard one any day.

'The wait's over, gorgeous. I can't imagine ever not loving you.'

She kissed him long and hard, taking full advantage of their shadowy corner, and let the slippery silk of her traditional wedding attire slide against the rich fabric of his. In it, he looked every bit a Bedouin.

'Think Salim would mind if we borrowed one

of his camels and just rode out into the desert?' she asked. The thought of galumphing along with her beautiful dress streaming out behind her and her arms wrapped tightly around his hard waist…

Brad laughed. 'Looking to indulge a few desert fantasies, Sera?'

'I have a lifetime of fantasies to fulfil,' she promised.

Brad traced the back of his hand across her cheek and drew her gaze into his own deep, dark one. 'Happy Christmas, Mrs Kruger.'

She twisted her hands more tightly behind his neck. 'Wow. That's going to take some getting used to.'

'Being Mrs Kruger?' he asked.

She pressed her mouth to his and then breathed against it. 'Being happy.'

So, this was what it felt like! As if someone had boiled up the colours of the desert into a delicious, golden tea and then given it to her to drink. It spread outward from her heart, warm and golden and immensely fulfilling.

'Are you up for it?'

With him by her side? She was up for anything. 'Totally.'

* * * * *